The Swamp

Bill Thomas

The Swamp

Special Consultants: **Dr. Gary Hendrix**
Dr. Don Whitehead

W · W · Norton & Company · Inc ·
New York

Other books by Bill Thomas: Tripping in America: Off the Beaten Track (1974)

Eastern Trips & Trails (1975)

Mid-America Trips & Trails (1975)

First published, 1976, in the United States by W. W. Norton & Company, Inc., New York. Published simultaneously in Canada by George J. McLeod Limited, Toronto.

All rights reserved under International and Pan-American Copyright Conventions. *Printed and bound by Dai Nippon Printing Co., Ltd.*, Tokyo, Japan.

Designed by Philip Sykes

First Edition

ISBN 0-393-08747-6

Contents

Acknowledgments

The author wishes to express a deep and abiding
appreciation to all those who so graciously gave their time,
advice, and effort to this work, including
Virginia Carter and Dr. Benjamin McPherson of the
U.S. Geological Survey; Dr. Gary Hendrix,
Fred and Sandy Dayhoff, Lew Cowardin, Dr. H. T. Odum,
Dr. Eugene Odum, Juanita Aga, Kenneth Morrison,
Mayor Leo Hance, Dr. Arthur Marshall, Chuck
and Janet Mason, Joseph Mazzoni, Dr. Minter
J. Westerfall, Jr., Bob Campbell, Jim Elder,
and Harry Hampton; Dr. Wade T. Batson,
Mrs. Frederick Bradford, Mrs. Marian Paoliello,
Tom Laveck, Ray Curran, Dr. Howard V. Weems, Jr.,
Dr. R. E. Woodruff, Dr. Frank W. Mead, Dr. George
Hageman, Dr. Fred G. Thompson, Dr. Don Whitehead,
Brooke Meanley, Larry and Dr. Suzanne Prather.

Ms. Sandra Thompson, Frank Davis, Ms. Dollie
Hoffman, Bernadette Monlezun, Dr. Charles Fryling,
Dr. Elmer Palmatier, Joice Veselka, Bob Hermes,
Dr. Iver Brook, Ms. Shirley Pomponi, Ben Moffett,
Debi Taylor, Dr. Frank Young, Norman Brunswig,
Doug Clayton, J. C. Truluck, John Dennis,
Wendell Metzen, Katherine Ewel, Prof. Lee Jenkins,
Brian Schofield, the late Desireé Steiner, Dorothy Scoville,
Jerry Cutlip, Ms. Pat Gammon, Mary Keith Garrett,
James Smith, Lloyd and Adele Beesley, Wyatt Moore,
Mike Watson, Holger Harvey, Fred Hudson,
Mrs. Florence Zuck, Dr. John Mulleedy, Jack Stark,
John Eadie, Byron Almquist, Connie Sherley, Joe
Newcomb, Gerald Clawson, Dr. Roy Clarkson, Betty
Bartholomew, Oscar and Phoebe Schubert, Tom Telfer,
Robert E. Nelson, Lee Hotchkiss, Frank Montalbano,
Dave Farlow, Greg Williams, and Dr. Z. S. Altschuler.
My special thanks to Phyllis and Alan Thomas,
to Bill Moore, and a host of others too numerous to mention.

To my editors—Starling Lawrence and James
Mairs—I offer a special note of appreciation,
for without them this book would never have come to be.

To Phyllis
who shares my love for all things
wild and beautiful

Prologue

Just as the beauty and usefulness of swamps have somehow eluded man through the ages, so have clear-cut definitions of just what a swamp is. The meaning of "swamp" may vary from region to region or from individual to individual. Even Webster's unabridged dictionary is vague in its description, saying a swamp is a "sponge, fungus, a term applied to spongy ground; low ground filled with water; soft, wet ground; a marsh; a bog."

The U.S. Geological Survey has been as remiss in defining a swamp as has Webster's; so has the U.S. Fish and Wildlife Service of the Department of the Interior. Only in 1975–76 did the Fish and Wildlife Service, which is constantly involved with wetland habitat for wildlife and waterfowl in America, establish a definition. Wildlife biologist Lewis Cowardin, who was instrumental in drawing up criteria for the project, said the agency considers as swamps all wetlands with greater than 50 percent area cover of woody plants. In other words, if a place has tree or bush growth and remains soggy or covered with a few inches of water on a permanent basis, it is generally considered a swamp.

"The woody vegetation," said Cowardin, "may be trees, shrubs or vines, or a mixture of all these. Swamps with trees often have an understory of shrubs and a ground layer of herb species. The herb species should not be strongly considered, however, as criteria for definition, for they are often the same or closely related to those found in marshes."

The marsh, on the other hand, is usually an area with high saline or alkaline content in the soil. Some are tidal and some are inland. To the layman, the marsh distinguishes itself most readily from the swamp by its vegetative cover, and is almost totally lacking in any bush or tree growth. Instead, here are found marsh grasses, bulrushes, cattails, spike grasses, and sedge. Usually the swamp has water standing or flowing through or over it; the marsh may or may not have apparent water, although the ground is soggy.

The bog bears much similarity to the swamp, but it is a quagmire dominated not by trees and woody plants, but instead by herbaceous plants as well as spaghnum and polytrichum moss. It may have some of the characteristics of both marsh and swamp, but generally the bog (which usually originates from an aging lake) is covered with growths of mosses, lichens, and ferns; little or no water is apparent until you step on it. The effect is much like stepping on a wet sponge, and the water readily gushes from it.

CHAPTER
1
The Swamp

What wonderful creatures we humans are, with
our eyes and minds—and almost infinite capacities.
How curious and sad that somewhere along the
line we seem to have lost our reverence and
understanding of the earth. We live so
much of our lives as aliens from the land. We war
on the land, pillage it, and try to bend it to
our will. And we diminish ourselves thereby, perhaps
far more than we know.

—Peggy Wayburn

From nearly the beginning, there was the swamp. Through it many forms of life evolved; it became a place of transition where the years of man were counted only as fleeting moments. Time was instead measured in millenia. It is difficult for those of us who live but moments in the eons of geologic cycles to comprehend the concept of eternity—or the time since the earth was born. But it is in those terms that the ages of the swamp are counted.

The lifeblood of the swamp is water. It begins—as a river begins—with a drop of rain. From the surrounding terrain it takes the drainage water; deep within the ground it taps into the seepage and etheral flows and generates new life within its own realm. Without water, the swamp would cease to be and its inhabitants would perish.

To visit the swamp is to travel backwards in time, to become, almost, a witness to creation. How many raindrops fell upon this place before man was born to measure time or count the sunrises and sunsets? The creation that is a continuing aspect of the swamp is an infinitely slow alchemy. While no one was present to chronicle the processes, scientists surmise it was some form of plant life that first ventured out of the sea onto land and made the changes that land existence requires. The first few plants that could live out of the water probably developed during the Silurian period, perhaps from algae in coastal areas that spread out onto moist soil alongside the water. And as they developed and grew, they became part of the process by which a swamp is born.

In keeping with its origins, the swamp today is still a breeding ground, a place of transition and growth, for many of the creatures of both land and sea. The pink shrimp, for instance, is dependent upon the estuaries and mangrove swamps of the Florida Everglades and the swamps and marshes of the Gulf for its birth and early growth. Some biologists believe the shrimp to be in a stage of evolutionary transition from the sea to land. There are, also, the terrestrial tendencies of a marine snail found in abundance in the marshes as well as on higher ground. Through the marsh and the swamp, the evolutionary processes may still be taking place. The rate is so infinitely slow that man finds it difficult to measure or even notice.

When Europeans discovered America and began to move into the continent, they skirted the swamps, for these were fearsome, mysterious places. There were few swamps in the old country, and many of those who came had never encountered such places before. Because the swamp was unknown to them, they feared it and stayed away. Then, when the other land was mostly settled, sporadic forays into the swamp by the more courageous revealed their natural resources and their potential. The swamp's fertility, they felt, would produce great agricultural crops if properly drained. There were ample supplies of timber, particularly cypress, which were in strong demand. Some swamps even produced minerals. During the Revolutionary War, for instance, bog iron by the ton was taken from the New Jersey wetlands. In later times, the swamps have been ideal places for expansion for housing projects and jetports. In many swamps, oil has been discovered, and some, including the Big Thicket and the Atchafalaya, are considerable producers.

11

Since virtually all swamps have a peat base, the early settlers naturally felt this dark black soil would grow just about anything. That wasn't necessarily true, as was discovered by farming efforts in the Great Dismal and the Okefenokee. But it wasn't before considerable damage was done to the swamp by efforts to drain it and turn it to the production of crops.

Nearly every swamp in America, great or small, has been subject to these pressures of civilization. Some of them, through accident of the natural terrain or difficulty of access, have survived. Others have been less fortunate. One of Florida's great swamps—Tate's Hell—in the panhandle section is virtually no more. Once covering thousands upon thousands of acres, a pond cypress and titi swamp through which a dog could scarcely pass, Tate's Hell was a beautiful, dense habitat for wildlife.

Today one can drive virtually throughout Tate's Hell Swamp. In the 1950s most of the land there was purchased by the Buckeye Cellulose Corp., a subsidiary of Proctor and Gamble, and the swamp has since been converted into a pine wood pulp plantation. Roads were built, canals dug and the swamp has disappeared, along with most of its inhabitants. The pristine beauty and the mysterious atmosphere no longer exist. And whatever role the swamp played in the ecology of northern Florida is also lost.

Although we may speak of the intrinsic values of the swamp, describe the strange beauty of its silent wooded chambers and watery prairies echoing the roar of the bull alligator or the call of the bald eagle, there is a practical aspect to its existence as well. Our values, unfortunately, must often be spelled out in tangible terms. Leaving aside the aesthetic dimension of the swamp and restricting our discussion to utility and cold cash, we must conclude that our civilization has been foolish and short-sighted in its destruction of swamplands.

We are only beginning to understand the practical value of the swamp and its ecology, but we know already that it is much easier and less expensive to preserve a swamp than to build one. In the 1960s, at a cost of $30 million, the Kissimmee River, which drains the area of Orlando, Florida was "improved" to accommodate the giant amusement complex of Disney World. Six dams were constructed, curves were straightened, the stream's length was shortened to fifty-eight miles, and some 40,000 acres of marsh were drained. The idea was to assist nature.

Disney World pioneered huge central Florida expansion, and with it came pollution. In 1975 the polluted Kissimmee flow into Lake Okeechobee threatened the water supply of south Florida. Scientists pointed out that the old river, in its meandering course through the swamps, had been able to cleanse itself of pollution. (For example, ecologists estimate that 1,500 acres of marsh can remove nitrogen and phosphates from the sewage of a city of 62,000 people.)

Consequently, in order to solve the problem, the Kissimmee may have to be taken back where it was. The stream may again be lengthened, the dams opened, the marshes and swamps restored at a cost to the taxpayers of at least $88 million. Scientists already are predicting a time when pure water will be the earth's most valuable and

12

1

3

1. *Many swamps include pools, which contain dense populations of game fish.*

2. *Female redwing blackbird.*

3. *The widow, one of the most common types of dragonfly found in the southeastern swamps.*

4

5

6

7

4. *Cattails, often commonly associated with marshes, also grow in some swamps, particularly along the borders.*

5. *A tiger swallowtail butterfly.*

6. *There are more than a dozen species and subspecies of praying mantis, one almost a foot in length. They devour other insects.*

7. *The water hyacinth, imported from Latin America, has become a dominant weed in southern streams; it has been found useful in purifying water.*

8. *Butterfly weed.*

9. *Thistles.*

10. *Fog or heavy dews, make spiderwebs more apparent to flying insects that might otherwise become entrapped.*

8

10

9

11. American bald eagle. Note the nest and eaglet in lower left corner.

12. Some species of fish and birds depend upon the mosquito as their main food source.

13. A bog in New Jersey's Pine Barrens.

11

12

scarcest natural resource. Already the water table in virtually all parts of the nation is considerably lower than it was just twenty-five years ago.

A study to determine feasible uses of swamps to break down sewage and purify water was carried out recently at the University of Florida through a joint grant from the Rockefeller Foundation and the National Science Foundation. The $1.4-million project, under the direction of Dr. Howard T. Odum, of the university, tested the hypothesis that a swamp can serve as a natural biological filter for the wastes generated by development. The test involved the piping of partially treated municipal sewage into the headwaters of two small cypress swamps. The polluted waters were then purified by the plants and peat accumulations and returned to the natural hydrologic cycle in the course of their slow progress seaward through the swamp. At the same time, the waste water's burden of nutrients was absorbed by the swamp ecosystem, enriching its capacity to sustain life.

There are still problems to be worked out. For instance, it has not yet been determined just what effect some of the heavy metals from the sewage will have on the swamps or upon plant and wildlife there. Also, the infusion of sewage has brought about an influx of foreign growth. Duckweed cover over all of one dome depleted oxygen to a point where it destroyed most fish and amphibian life. Other weeds such as fireweed and dog fennel (a rampant weed that dominates most other growth) became prominent on some of the hammocks in the domes.

Since there are large numbers of small cypress dome swamps ranging from one to twenty-five acres in size in Florida (as many as 40,000 of them in some counties), their use for purification of sewage, for recycling water, could be quite valuable in keeping our earth clean and livable. Katherine Ewel, a research associate of Dr. Odum's, said the generally accepted evaluation is that a swamp with flowing waters—even very slowly flowing waters—would provide greater recycling powers than a swamp that had no flow at all.

Similar tests were conducted during a research project in the Florida Everglades by Dr. Kerry Steward, of the U.S. Department of Agriculture, as part of a south Florida ecological study. His report shows that the Everglades could renovate waste water if the system could assimilate substances dissolved in the water without adversely affecting the environment. Sawgrass plants, however, because of their low nutrient requirement, have a limited capacity for removing nutrients from the water and therefore could probably not be used efficiently to renovate waste water.

In Mississippi, the National Aeronautic and Space Administration (NASA) was carrying out some experiments under its environmental program in swamps and bayous choked with water hyacinths. Although hyacinths are an exotic plant imported from Latin America and considered a major nuisance in southern waters, they are nevertheless an integral part of the environment of many southern swamps today. NASA found that the hyacinths play a great role in recycling and purifying sewage. On one side of a small swamp, NASA injected a stream of sewage that had already undergone treatment, breaking it down into a liquid state so that it would flow through a thick mat of water hyacinths. Just 400 feet away, tests were made of the water. Result: The water was checked by the local health department and found pure enough to drink, purer, in fact, than many cities' present drinking-water supplies. The water hyacinths not only do the job effectively, but at considerably less cost than any other known system.

The principle of purification is fairly simple. In fact, it is already being used by a small town in northeast Georgia (Braselton) not in a swamp, but on a tilted, wooded hillside with a 35 percent slope. The town of 500 residents was faced with a sewage problem after the existing plant failed, so it copied the idea from towns in Europe, which had long been successfully using such systems, of spraying the sewage from sprinkler systems in a deep woods. The town gives its sewage secondary treatment, which removes about 85 percent of the pollutants, before spraying it into the wooded area. The water then sinks into the ground and is purified before being released into nearby streams. By the time it gets to the streams, it is actually purer than it was originally.

Dr. Wade Nutter of the School of Forest Resources at the University of Georgia researched the idea before it was put into effect at Braselton. "It works and works well," he said. "And the cost is only a percentage of that used by other treatment systems. There are examples in Europe of such systems over a hundred years old. The most famous one in the world probably is in Melbourne, Australia, a twenty-eight-thousand-acre site where they treat all their sewage for slightly over one dollar per person per year. I see no reason why such a system would not work just as well or better in swamps."

NASA also found hyacinths can be used for cattle feed as well as the manufacture of natural gas for heating. According to a spokesman for NASA's National Space Technology Laboratories, a few acres of hyacinths could produce enough natural gas for a city of 30,000 people. And since swamps are natural habitat for water hyacinths (the Atchafalaya and Honey Island Swamps of Louisiana are filled with them), this may become another important function of the swamp environment.

In an effort to save the Alcovy River Swamp from a channeling and draining project by the U.S. Soil Conservation Service, Dr. Charles Wharton of Georgia State University has attempted to express the intangible values of the swamp in terms of dollars and cents. Dr. Wharton set out to show how much the state of Georgia would lose financially if it should authorize the proposed channeling of the 2,300-acre swamp, located just thirty miles southeast of Atlanta. Calculating all kinds of useful yields of the swamp to the people of the Atlanta area (education, water quality and quantity, recreation, and general harvestable production), he projected a total annual value of $7,189,103 and a 100-year value of $403,019,333; that was before the skyrocketing inflationary period of the mid-1970s.

"I tried to bring together enough evidence to make it clear that the river swamp has important values now and in the future," he said.

13

14. (Overleaf) Because of its tolerance for water, the cypress tree is found in virtually all swamps of the Southeast, extending from Delaware to the Texas Big Thicket.

17

Dr. Wharton's estimated economic value of the Alcovy Swamp included $5.4-million a year for education, ranging from public school system use and public visits to graduate dissertations and research. By recharging underground supplies of fresh water, he estimated the swamp contributes $228,000 a year to Atlanta. In purifying river and lake water, the swamp is worth $1 million annually. He computed the productive value of the swamp in terms of lumber and building topsoil at $550,000 annually. His study did not undertake an estimate of the value of wildlife supported by the Alcovy.

"It's a sad commentary upon our society that one has to use such tactics to save original landscape," said Dr. Archie Carr, research ecologist at the University of Florida. "But," he added, "it apparently works . . . for the Alcovy was spared."

Since pioneer times, the American attitude towards the swamp has been one of indifference bordering on hostility. The swamp has even been subjected to legislative attack. In the middle of the nineteenth century, the Congress passed three acts known as the Swamp Land Acts of 1849, 1850, and 1860. The Swamp Land Act of 1849 granted to Louisiana all swamp and overflow lands then unfit for cultivation, the object being to help in controlling floods in the Mississippi River Valley. And just a year later, the act of 1850 was made applicable to another twelve states having lands of public domain within their boundaries. In 1860 its provisions were extended to Oregon and Minnesota.

The original purpose of the grants enabled the states to reclaim their wetlands by the construction of levees and drains. The state, it was hoped, would enact programs to reclaim the land and eliminate mosquito-breeding swamps. By the mid-1950s, nearly sixty-five million acres had been patented to the fifteen states, and minor adjustments are still underway. Swamplands were never ceded to the other nineteen states then holding public lands (lands which had never been claimed by a private individual and remained in public trust).

A good example of what happened after the lands were ceded to the states is Iowa. Here the land was turned over to the counties where it was bartered for all sorts of considerations such as public buildings and bridges. Some counties bargained with immigration companies, selling land to a company for twenty-five to seventy-five cents an acre with the provision that the company put settlers on the land. In other cases, the land was sold by county commissioners to themselves for nominal considerations. Of the sixty-five million acres given to the states, nearly all are now in private ownership. And the federal and state agencies are, with taxpayers' money, trying to purchase many of these so-called wastelands back at high prices.

Nonetheless, the swamp remains one of the last frontiers of true wilderness in many parts of America. In fact, those that have survived have been noticeably less affected by the pressures of civilization than any other part of the landscape. At one time, nearly an eighth of the nation consisted of swamp, marsh, or bog. Many of the great swamps long ago disappeared. One of the largest swamps in all of mid-America—the Limberlost, immortalized by

novelist Gene Stratton-Porter in 1909—covered several thousand acres. Today it has been converted to farmland.

Many of the great swamps still remaining, if left alone, will likely survive the ages, perhaps to remain the lone sanctuaries of beauty and the beast, places where nature may take its course unaltered and unguided by the will of man. The Four Holes in South Carolina is a prime example. In other places, the swamp as it exists today could not long endure were it not assisted by man. The Corkscrew Swamp in Florida, for instance, had it not been for efforts by the National Audubon Society, would already have disappeared. The Big Cypress, perhaps America's most molested and abused swamp, was well on its way to vanishing before being designated by Congress as a National Water Preserve.

The swamps are changing. Over the past half-century we have lost many of them to the economic interests of man; a great many others likely will be lost before the turn of the century. The Atchafalaya in Louisiana, America's third largest swamp, is disappearing and may do so regardless of what man does to save it. The upper reaches of the Atchafalaya once stretched from Arkansas all the way to the Gulf. Today the northern third of that swamp is farmland, and the rest is rapidly filling with silt deposits from the Mississippi and its tributaries.

The swamp is, in a sense, an endangered species. It plays a central role in the survival of creatures which inhabit it, and, as we shall see, it is far more important to our survival than we realize. The swamp is indeed a fragile environment, and life here depends on a tenuous balance of soil, water, sun, and wind. The tolerances are slight; the swamp can easily be destroyed either by man's indifference or, on the other extreme, by his overzealous enthusiasm. Aldo Leopold, an early American conservationist, once described the problem thus: " . . . to cherish we must see and fondle, and when enough have seen and fondled, there is no wilderness left to cherish."

A flight over that portion of the Florida Everglades north of the Tamiami Trail shows tracks across the land in every direction, left there by airboats. In the Big Cypress there are ruts left by swamp buggies carrying people into the inner sanctum of the swamp. Neither of these places has seen much protection over the years. But the scars do not end there. From the airplane one can also see the tracks left by footsteps in that portion included in the Everglades National Park, paths worn across the sawgrass prairie by people visiting the hammocks or participating in what the National Park Service calls the "Swamp Tromp."

The Park Service is aware of the damage, of course, but feels it is offset by intimately acquainting more people with the Glades. "We need for people to know what it's like," one ranger said, "so perhaps they'll have a greater appreciation for it and will, in time, help by bringing pressure to bear on politicians to insure its preservation." Perhaps they are right, however sad that it should be so.

Were we to follow an open-door policy to the swamps, strip them and convert every possible asset to money, those riches would soon be gone, forgotten—and with them, the swamp itself. What's more, we would still be in need. For by using these resources, we are merely buying time selfishly for our own generation and perhaps a generation or two to follow. The oil deposits, the peat, the trees will soon be depleted, and we will be forced to turn elsewhere for resource substitutes.

Even during the middle of the nineteenth century, there were those with enough wisdom and foresight to see what was happening to our land. Among them was Chief Seattle of the Duwanish tribe, who voiced his concern and prophesied the following in a letter to President Franklin Pierce in 1855:

"The whites, too, shall pass—perhaps sooner than other tribes. Continue to contaminate your bed, and you will one night suffocate in your own waste. When the buffalo are all slaughtered, the wild horses all tamed, the secret corners of the forest heavy with the scent of many men, and the views of the ripe hills blotted by talking wires. Where is the thicket? Gone. Where is the eagle? Gone. And what is it to say good bye, to the swift and the hunt, the end of living and the beginning of survival?"

The beginning of survival is already, it would seem, upon us. Many of the creatures that inhabited the earth in 1855 no longer exist. As time passes, more and more creatures of the wild are placed upon the endangered species list compiled by the U.S. Department of the Interior. Instead, we convert the earth to concrete, the air and water to poison, the solitude to noise.

"There is no quiet place in the white man's cities," Chief Seattle continued. "No place to hear the leaves of spring or the rustle of insect wings. But perhaps because I am savage and do not understand, the clatter seems to insult the ears. And what is there to life if a man cannot hear the lovely cry of the whippoorwill or the arguments of the frogs around the pond at night."

We have not yet educated our people to the values of the swamp. Neither have we yet framed effective laws to control destruction and abuse of the swamp, nor are we likely to do so until we understand more about it and its creatures. And that is in large measure my reason for writing this book. For by looking more closely into the mysteries of this place we begin to perceive the ties that link us as human beings at one end of the evolutionary scale to such creatures as the reptile and the mosquito at the other end. It is a chain that we ignore at our own period, for as Peggy Wayburn points out in *The Edge of Life:* "The earth does not belong to us; we belong to it. We are subject to the same immutable laws that govern all living things. We are no more in ultimate control of the earth than we are of our own life-spans."

15

16

15. *Gas forms bubbles under algae on an Indiana swamp.*

16. *Algae caught on cattail blades.*

17. *Duckweed is found on many pools where the flow of water is either slow or nonexistent.*

18. *Baby tadpoles are choice food for wading birds and fish.*

19. *A small bullfrog keeps one eye out for flying insects which will provide him with a meal, the other for predators which would have him for a meal.*

17

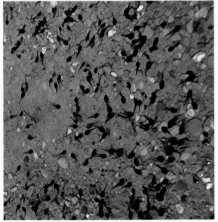

18

19

CHAPTER

2

The Great Swamp of New Jersey

When from our better selves we have too long
Been parted by the hurrying world, and droop,
Sick of its business, of its pleasures tired,
How Gracious, how benign, is Solitude.

—William Wordsworth

Suddenly the New Jersey landscape blossomed into open space blanketed by a pale waist-high layer of ground fog. Dense woodlands and open meadows, lush and green as the tropics, replaced the scramble of closely crowded rows of suburbia. The hum of traffic faded into the distance.

The Great Swamp, particularly at daybreak on a rainy June morning, is an unexpected and pleasant surprise in the midst of the world's greatest megalopolis. Just beyond the horizon to the east (less than thirty miles as the crow flies) is New York City's Times Square. Seven miles to the north is Morristown, N.J. But here, the urban world, as if by magic, is swept from view.

Near the roadside, in a meadow carpeted with seeding grass, were three white-tailed doe, their heads raised and ears flicking with curiosity at my intrusion. Satisfied I was a creature of no particular concern to them, they returned to grazing. The Great Swamp is a haven for many species of wildlife, as well as a place of convenient escape for man.

One need travel only a short distance into the backwoods of the Great Swamp to become lost in as primeval a wilderness as any to be found in America. Somehow, despite the pressures of civilization and what is commonly called progress, it has survived, a rare gem in the midst of elbow-to-elbow humanity. Today its preservation is assured; it is managed as a national wildlife refuge by the U.S. Fish and Wildlife Service of the Department of the Interior. Not so many years ago, however, the future of the Great Swamp looked grim indeed. Except for some concerted efforts upon the parts of several courageous people, the Great Swamp might this day be a great metropolitan jetport.

Among those to campaign for the swamp's survival were Dr. Bob Zuck and his wife, Florence, both of whom teach at nearby Drew University. The Zucks had spent years of their life in the swamp, studying its flora, enjoying its serene atmosphere, and utilizing it as an outdoor classroom and laboratory. Prior to December 1959, the Zucks had taken the Great Swamp for granted.

Then the New York Port Authority announced its plans to build a jetport right in the middle of the river birch, crack willow, and the reflecting pools of the Great Swamp. Kennedy, La Guardia, and Newark Airports were no longer sufficient to handle all New York traffic, and the Port Authority, forced to look for more room to expand, saw the Great Swamp as an answer to its problems.

From the Port Authority's point of view, here was 6,000 acres of open, worthless real estate that would never be missed. Before anyone realized it, the conversion would be history. They did not count on the magnitude of the ensuing controversy, however. The Zucks were among thousands of local people who banded together as the Great Swamp Committee of the North American Wildlife Federation. Money was raised, real estate was purchased or donated by willing landowners, and in 1960 nearly 3,000 acres were presented as a gift from the local people to the U.S. Fish and Wildlife Service.

This was the beginning of the Great Swamp National

1

2

3

1. *Cinnamon fern is easily identified at this stage in the spring by its brown sporophylls.*

2. *A common eastern water snake relaxes amid camouflage of duckweed on some submerged tree limbs.*

3. *A sedge (center) is surrounded by sensitive and cinnamon ferns.*

4. *A nature trail across a pond via this elevated boardwalk allows visitors the opportunity to become a part of the swamp environment and study it close up.*

4

Wildlife Refuge. Since that time, considerably more land has been acquired by the federal government, a continuing project to achieve a goal of 6,000 acres. And what was considered in the mid-fifties by the Port Authority to be a piece of worthless real estate is today a priceless retreat for man, bird, and beast.

Prior to 1959, most of the swamp's neighbors either ignored or shunned it. To them it was a place occupied by swarms of fierce mosquitoes and black flies which made life unbearable, where snakes coiled upon tree limbs to strike the hiker in the neck, where one might become entrapped in quicksand and sink from sight within a few hours. But attitudes, partially because of that controversy and the dissemination of information about the Great Swamp, have changed. Now people no longer take it for granted; they're immensely interested in the swamp and its inhabitants.

Said Mrs. Zuck: "The poised dagger of the Port Authority forced all of us to take a new look at the swamp. Only then did we begin to fully realize just what it meant to everyone . . . and more importantly, what it would mean to the many generations to come."

Had the Port Authority failed to move, the Great Swamp might ultimately have died anyway. One has merely to study the fringe areas to note the signs of death—junked automobiles, housing subdivisions, garbage dumps. The streams—the Passaic River, Black Brook, and Great Brook—were cluttered with rubbish, their banks a sodden mess of strewn papers, rusted cans, and plastic containers. The swamp was actually dying; its demise would have gone largely unnoticed. The swamp had been there forever; no one could imagine it disappearing.

A hundred million years or so ago when the land was still being formed, volcanoes spewed great successive waves of lava to create the Watchung Mountains on the south and east. Draining the lava hills was the Passaic River. Then came the Wisconsin Glacier about 40,000 years ago, cutting off the stream and forcing it to flow southward. As the ice melted and the glacier retreated some 20,000 years later, the prehistoric Lake Passaic, covering an area thirty miles long and ten miles wide, was formed. Through the ages the lake disappeared, leaving a sodden bowl which became the Great Swamp. The new path of the Passaic River wound east of Long Hill, a rocky rise 450 to 500 feet above the eastern edge of the Great Swamp; Great Brook and Black Brook now drain the area to the west until they, too, join the Passaic.

Along the low banks of the brooks are wetlands, subject to recurrent flooding. And in others where the elevation gained as much as two feet, handsome hardwood trees grow—hickories, beeches, maples, oaks, and elms. The glacier created a transition community of plants which represented both northern and southern zones; they'd been planted by the glacier and have continued to propagate themselves through the ages. Wild azalea, laurel, pepperbush, and rhododendron grow next to marsh marigold, spatterdock, lizards-tail, and skunk cabbage.

The core of the swamp has remained basically unchanged, but history tells us there have been some alterations. John W. Barber and Henry Howe wrote in their *Historical Collections of the State of New Jersey* in 1844:

"The whole was, until recently, covered by a heavy growth of timber. About one half of the tract is cleared, and drained by ditches, and near the upland is susceptible of tillage, the rest being excellent meadows, producing very large crops of good 'foul meadow' hay. In the upper or eastern section is a very large tract of turf of peat, suitable for fuel, of various depths. . . . In the midst, and throughout the whole swamp, there are numerous ridges of dry land rising like islands, of a sandy soil, and those uncleared are covered with chestnut timber."

The chestnut trees, of course, have disappeared because of the dread chestnut blight; and timber barons saw that many of the other forested areas of the swamp did also.

The Great Swamp is not merely a swamp—it is a paradox. While there are huge areas of swampland and wetlands, there are also marshes and meadows; dry, elevated wooded ridges, and small areas of magnificent virgin timber. Cattails contrast beautifully with huge stands of mountain laurel, wild orchids, mayflowers, ferns, and rhododendron.

"My husband and I have been working on cataloguing the plants of the Great Swamp," explained Mrs. Zuck. "We believe there may be as many as a thousand species to be found here. Among them are twenty-three types of moss, sixteen ferns, seven kinds of goldenrod, nine different asters, and a large number of grasses and sedges. It is, we feel, a botanical paradise of great scientific and esthetic value. I suppose those who love to watch wildlife treasure it equally as much for its animal population."

Birdwatchers come from many miles around the swamp to walk the nature trails and boardwalks, binoculars and identification books in hand. The Great Swamp is located just south of a point where the Hudson River and Atlantic Flyways merge; thus it is an important feeding area and resting place for migratory waterfowl and passerine birds. More than 180 species of bird life have been recorded by ornithologists, among them pintails and wood ducks; red-headed and pileated woodpeckers; barred, great horned, and saw-whet owls; long-billed marsh wrens and American bitterns; herons, egrets, rails, coots, and gallinules.

The U.S. Fish and Wildlife Service manages the swamp primarily as a wildlife refuge. But it has perhaps the heaviest concentration of visitors of any national wildlife refuge in the country. Just ten years after it was established, there were more than a quarter-million visitors, and that figure increases dramatically year by year.

The Great Swamp is a bit of backwoods Americana tucked neatly into the folds of megalopolis. Before the wildlife refuge was established, coon hunters came here to sit with their backs against an oak on a cold night under a harvest moon and listen to the sounds of dogs running somewhere in the morass; they would swap stories, reminiscing about great dogs which bugled through the swamp generations before them. Blueberry pickers in July will risk mosquitoes, soaked feet, and the possibility of getting lost; but the thought of giant blueberry bushes overburdened with rich blue fruit is too much for them to resist.

5. *During the early morning and again late in the evening, white-tailed deer emerge from the thickets to graze in the meadows.*

6. *River* Equisetum, *one of the botanical prizes of the Great Swamp, grows in shallow water.*

6

7

8

9

7. *A pair of wood ducks feed among sedges during the late evening.*

8. *A family of Canada geese.*

9. *Dense growth of arrowhead along a stream leading out of the Great Swamp.*

10. *A Canada goose keeps a wary eye out for would-be predators while her goslings feed.*

10

On one corner of the swamp is an outdoor education center operated by the Morris County Park Commission, and it's through here that many young visitors first become acquainted with the Great Swamp. In July and August the outdoor education center is closed because of mosquitoes and in order to give the plants a chance to root and recover; for the remainder of the year, the center is open seven days a week. A museum marks the headquarters, but the primary point of interest is a one-mile combination trail and boardwalk through the swamp. Because this trail leads through territory more varied and with greater plant growth than any other point in the swamp, it's a good place to gain an understanding of what the swamp is all about; then one can pursue his or her own particular interests.

In 1968 the Great Swamp won another distinction by becoming the first National Wildlife Refuge to be included in the National Wilderness Preservation System. At that time, Congress designated the eastern two-thirds of the refuge, a total of 3,750 acres, as an area to remain "forever wild." As a result, no manmade structures or motorized vehicles and equipment are allowed. Roads were closed, but remain as hiking trails. No camping is allowed here or at any other place on the refuge, and regulations prohibit visitors on the premises before sunrise or after dusk. But for those who are legitimate watchers of wildlife and find themselves still at the blinds as the moon rises, regulations are tempered with flexibility.

As I traveled along the backroads of the refuge perimeter my last day in the swamp, pausing here and there to harvest the view which unfolded before me, I pondered: How far does one have to travel to meet the miracle of life—all the way around the world at the speed of sound? Does it lie along the coral reef of the El Camino Real or across the Bering Strait at Little Diomede? Thoreau, in his journal, says no further than "here." And "here" at this particular moment happened to be a brief view of Great Brook, framed with lily pads and a forest curtain that crowded close and arched above like a great natural cathedral. One knows after such a sojourn, however brief, in the Great Swamp that quality of life both begins and ends here, that the values of the Great Swamp to mankind are, in fact, limitless.

CHAPTER
3
The Great Dismal Swamp

Away to the Dismal Swamp he speeds;
His Path was rugged and sore;
Through tangled juniper, beds of reeds,
Through many a fen, where the serpent feeds,
And never man trod before.

—Thomas Moore

In the shallows of Lake Drummond they stand like aged sentinels, their services spent—great bald cypress, their limbs crooked against the sky. These monarchs of the Great Dismal Swamp predate the birth of America; some may be as much as 1,600 years old. From their vantage point, the Dismal Swamp spreads in every direction, from horizon to horizon.

The Great Dismal, sprawled across the Virginia–North Carolina border tidewater country at the southern doorstep of the Norfolk-Chesapeake-Suffolk-Newport News-Virginia Beach megalopolis, is a place of legend and mystery. A sprinkling of great trees, with trunks deterio rated by the ages and washed away by the sweet, dark waters of Lake Drummond, is virtually all that remains of the great forest that once covered the swamp. Cypress still exist in the Great Dismal, scattered lightly throughout the swamp's expanse, but they are only shadows of what was once a primeval cypress forest.

Some 49,000 acres of this 750–square mile tangle of wilderness is owned by the Department of the Interior and operated as The Great Dismal Swamp National Wildlife Refuge. In an unprecedented move, the land was presented to the department in early 1973 by the Union Camp Corporation, a paper company which had had extensive land holdings in the area since before the turn of this century. It did so after years of pressure by conservation groups from across America.

In formal presentation ceremonies, Samuel Kinney, Jr., president of Union Camp, put this portion of the swamp's future in proper perspective: "This represents not only the best use but the only right use for our Dismal Swamp landholdings. The swamp's ecological significance and its wealth of history and lore make it a unique wilderness—one of the last, large wild areas remaining in the East." The presentation was made through the Nature Conservancy.

Lake Drummond, lying just north of center of the swamp, is considered by many the source of life here. While that may be true in some ways, the actual water supply for the Dismal flows from the highest point of the swamp—the Suffolk Scarp along the western edge— generally eastward. Its water is believed to come from an extensive underground water source known as the Norfolk aquifer, although some drainage water also spills into the swamp. The entire swamp is underlaid with peat, and some fear it may someday be mined, despite efforts to preserve the swamp in its present form.

The origin of Lake Drummond is somewhat in dispute. Some claim it was created by a great meteorite similar to those believed to have created the Carolina Bays (see Chapter 8), but others claim it was instead the result of a great underground peat burn somewhere between 3,500 to 6,000 years ago. It is oval-shaped, similar to the impact of a meteor, but Dr. Don Whitehead, an ecologist at Indiana University who did extensive studies of the swamp in the 1960s, claims the peat burn theory could be just as logical.

Lake Drummond is indeed the center of activity in the swamp today, however, with heavy use by fishermen, sightseers, and boaters. Boat tours for visitors are offered from the Dismal Swamp Canal to Lake Drummond.

1. *A great barred owl scans the swamp floor. Other species found here are wood duck, the pileated woodpecker, and the prothonotary warbler.*

2. *The tannin from trees and decaying matter dyes the waters of the Dismal the color of root beer. Early sailing ships carried water from the Dismal in casks to be used at sea, for it was felt the water had medicinal qualities.*

3. *Ivy vines clinging to a cypress stump begin to turn in late summer.*

4. *The Great Dismal is laced with canals which drain out the swamp, such as the Jericho Ditch.*

1

2

4

3

Although the swamp boundaries are rather well defined by the surrounding urban settlements, it's a surprising place of wilderness. It is a different kind of swamp; rather than a catch basin of stagnant pools, it's a gently flowing fountain. It harbors a fantastic array of plants, some of the last black bear east of the Appalachians, bobcat and possibly panther, some large copperheads and rattlesnakes.

Its soil burns; its water boasts the color and clarity of brandy; and some consider it wilder than the Florida Everglades. Many naturalists believe it to be our most valuable laboratory. It's a place of beauty and subtle danger, a veritable jungle. Few people have explored some of its farther reaches, and many of those who did muster the courage once would never return again.

Northern and southern plants grow side by side here in this botanical melting pot—magnolia, myrtle, jasmine, and cherry trees flourish beside switch cane, a native bamboo-type plant. There's jewel weed and gerardia, huge vines of the muscadine grape which in late summer produce a delicious fruit, the rare log fern and the devil's walking stick, sometimes known as Hercules's club.

The Great Dismal is a southern swamp, the northernmost of a great string along the Atlantic Coast that includes the Everglades and the Big Cypress in Florida, the Okefenokee, the Congaree and Four Holes swamps of South Carolina, and some of the Carolina Bays.

Among the swamp residents are a great variety of insects, including the greatest aggravator of outdoorsmen in the South—the red bug. Many of the oldtimers in and around the swamp, however, claim that "After you've been here awhile and acquired that swamp odor, red bugs don't bother you much." Others include yellow flies, mosquitoes, and a variety of ticks and butterflies. (In 1939, lepidopterist Austin Clark published a list of seventy three species collected in the northwest corner of the swamp—that portion now occupied as a national wildlife refuge.)

In the waters of Lake Drummond, the ditches and canals, are yellow perch, catfish, and a strange little sunfish called the flier by the local folk. Black crappies and redfin pickerel also live in Lake Drummond. No doubt the oddest creature is the Dismal Swamp fish, a member of the blindfish family usually found only in subterranean waterways.

Perhaps the most notable feature of the Great Dismal is the colored water, stained by tannin from the barks of trees. In fact, there are three distinct types of dark waters in the Dismal—juniper water (coffee-colored in Lake Drummond and the canals, but orange to chrome yellow in a glass); gum water (which looks like root beer from the dyes of gum roots and bark); and cypress water (the color of strong tea). An attempt was made at one time to stock the waters of Lake Drummond, which is no more than eleven feet deep at any point, with black bass; but the acidity in the water plus limited food supplies soon eliminated them.

Just when the Great Dismal Swamp was discovered, or by whom, has never been documented. It may have been by those who first settled this part of the country, for it is situated about halfway between the first two English col-

5

6

7

8

9

5. *This yellow-flowering plant is jewel weed, sometimes called touch-me-not.*

6. *The log fern is one of several species of fern found in the Great Dismal. Others include the netted chain fern (7), cinnamon and royal ferns. The Virginia chain fern (10) is common here.*

8. *Muscadine grapes ripen in the mid- to late summer and are sought after by opposums, raccoons, birds, and man.*

9. *Commonly called cane, this member of the bamboo family grows in cleared areas of the Dismal.*

onies in the New World: Jamestown and Fort Raleigh. But since the early settlers were busy just staying alive it seems likely they never ventured into the swamp. Before the coming of the white man, the Nansemond Indians occasionally hunted here until a diminishing game supply caused them to move elsewhere.

One early hunting expedition included William Drummond, the first colonial governor of North Carolina (1663–1667); but the party, like so many to come in later years, became hopelessly lost. After days of wandering about the swamp, Drummond found his way out, but his companions perished. One story goes that, during that expedition, the group stumbled upon what is now Lake Drummond and named it after the governor.

Colonel William Byrd II, who wrote the *Historie of the Dividing Line Betwixt Virginia and North Carolina,* is credited with giving the swamp its name. He described the swamp as a "horrible desert, the foul damps ascend without ceasing, corrupt the air and render it unfit for respiration . . . Never was Rum, that cordial of Life, found more necessary than in this Dirty Place."

Like many swamps, the Great Dismal from the beginning of the white man's presence on the continent, was threatened. A number of attempts have been made through the centuries to tame parts of the Great Dismal; each without exception has failed, including one by George Washington. In 1763 Washington and a group of wealthy Virginia planters formed a land corporation called the Dismal Swamp Land Co. which claimed 40,000 acres of the richest land as its own. They secured permission from Virginia to drain their land with canals and, with slave labor, cut a five-mile ditch from the western edge of the swamp to Lake Drummond. The canal is still there today.

The exact purpose of this canal has never been established by historians, but it is felt it was primarily an effort to drain the western portion of the swamp for agriculture. The canal worked, but the farming operation didn't. For try as he might, Washington was never able to get the rich peat soil to produce cotton and rice as he had envisioned. He found peat lacked the fertile ingredients necessary for producing crops and ultimately he gave up his dream.

A year after Washington's company failed, another group of businessmen headed by Patrick Henry formed a company and proposed that a canal be built through the swamp between the Norfolk Harbor and Albemarle Sound. The digging was slow and progress laborious. It took nearly thirty years to build that canal, and in 1814 the first ship made the twenty-two–mile trip through the Dismal Swamp Canal from Scotland Neck, N.C., to Norfolk. Since that time a number of canals—Railroad Ditch, Washington Ditch, Jericho Canal, South Ditch, Portsmouth Ditch, Hudnell Canal, and others—have been cut into the midst of the swamp.

After efforts to drain the swamp for agricultural purposes failed, timber companies moved in, cutting many of the giant cypress and white cedar for shipbuilding, as well as water gum and black gum for other construction. The result is a second forest growth that is radically changed. Instead of stands of cypress and gum, red maple, tulip tree, sweet bay, and pine now predominate the swamp.

11. Feelers from wild grapevines reach out for each other.

12. (Overleaf) Cypress grows out into the shallow water along the shoreline of Lake Drummond.

13. (Overleaf) Great cypress trees in Lake Drummond; believed to have been standing when America was discovered.

10

11

It's the hope of the U.S. Fish and Wildlife Service, which manages the refuge, to stabilize the highly altered ecosystem and encourage the regeneration of some of the original dominant species.

During the Civil War, the Great Dismal played still another role, as a place of refuge for runaway slaves from the surrounding area. Some estimates claim at least a thousand slaves lived within the swamp. Some of them worked making shingles from the bald cypress which they exchanged for supplies and food. The population became so great that dogs were employed to help the slave owners go in and hunt down their quarry. The bloody armed hunts became so outrageous that Henry Wadsworth Longfellow in 1842 wrote a poem, ''The Slave in the Dismal Swamp.''

> In dark fens of the Dismal Swamp
>> The hunted Negro lay;
> He saw the fire of the midnight camp,
> And heard at times a horse's tramp
>> And a bloodhound's distant bay.

In 1839 Harriet Beecher Stowe wrote *A Tale of the Great Dismal Swamp,* a novel about an escaped slave hiding out in the swamp, which she regarded as superior to *Uncle Tom's Cabin,* but which had a lesser impact upon society.

Another poet—Thomas Moore—wrote of the Great Dismal before Longfellow or Stowe. In the early 1800s he composed the ''Lake of the Dismal Swamp,'' a poem about a legendary Indian maiden whose ghost is reportedly seen to this day paddling a white canoe along the misty waterways.

Moore's poem tells how a bereaved Indian lover came to believe his lost love had departed her grave and taken to the swamp. He followed her and never returned but was reunited with his Lady of the Lake in death:

> But oft, from the Indian hunter's camp
>> This lover and maid so true
> Are seen at the hour of the midnight damp
> To cross the Lake by a fire-fly lamp,
>> And paddle their white canoe.

Through the years many a hunter and fisherman in the Great Dismal have claimed they have sighted the ghostly white canoe with its firefly lamp. Eerie lights are in fact not an uncommon sight in the swamp, but they are created by smoldering peat, burning methane escaping from decomposing vegetation, or from foxfire.

Somehow, the swamp has always attracted writers, but for different reasons. According to a biographer of Robert Frost, the young poet, suffering the rejection of a small book of poems from editor Elinor White, visited the swamp with the intent of ending his life there. Frost traveled from Boston to New York and then to Norfolk by train and steamer, then by carriage and on foot until he reached the Great Dismal. Having been impressed by the accounts of Moore and Longfellow, he decided this would be a most fitting place for the deed. But instead of plunging suicidally into the swamp, he trekked down the Dismal Swamp Canal towpath and continued on to Kitty Hawk and Hatteras. Things must not have been as bad as they

14

15

16

14. *The blackish berries of devil's walking stick mark the autumn harvest in the Dismal. The thorns of the walking stick make travel at night through the swamp a painful experience.*

15. *Wild purple gardenias bloom during the early autumn.*

16. *The seed pods of a type of reed found in the Dismal* (Erianthus gigamev).

seemed at the moment, for Elinor White later became Mrs. Robert Frost.

English writer Charles Frederick Stansbury described the Dismal as a place in which the imagination played strange tricks upon its victim. Imagine yourself wandering through the Dismal Swamp at night, he said, with briars and thorns tearing at your clothing and flesh, worrying about quicksand, mires, venomous snakes, and prowling bears and panthers. Suddenly you see a strange glow through the trees. Probably the most comforting thing you can think of is that long-dead Indian maiden peacefully paddling her canoe.

The refuge is open to the public for walking at any time of the year between sunrise and sunset, but proceed with caution. For there are poisonous snakes in the swamp, including the canebrake rattlesnake, the southern copperhead, and the cottonmouth moccasin.

Brooke Meanley, a biologist at the U.S. Fish and Wildlife Service's Patuxent Wildlife Research Center in Maryland, a noted authority on the Great Dismal, says about seventy-five species of birds are known to nest in the swamp, with a larger number of transients. Each winter, some twenty-five million blackbirds (redwing, common and boat-tailed grackles, and rusty blackbirds) invade the swamp. Also found here are wood duck, the pileated woodpecker, and the prothonotary warbler.

While there is some evidence of the swamp drying out, it will take many, many years for it to do so. It is a place of unusual hydrogeologic conditions, considering the extensive canal system which tends to drain off water from the soil. In many respects the Great Dismal Swamp appears to be an accident of nature, combining in one contiguous area a mixture of separate ecosystems, portions of those found in the East and Midwest, North and South. And it is this fact, more than any other, that differentiates it from nearly all other swamps in the eastern United States.

Although a major portion of the swamp is now under the protective management of the U.S. Fish and Wildlife Service, timber cutting continues in other parts of it, particularly in North Carolina. Ecologically and geologically, Dismal Swamp remains a wonderful and mysterious place whose secrets are still fairly well kept from man. But that's what makes it interesting.

CHAPTER
4
The Great Swamp of Rhode Island

The sky was blue and bare, but sun and sky were lost in that intense morass. From the black pools beneath bubbled the yellow breath of age, fouling the air.

—Paul Petrie

The hint of autumn was in the air. Red and golden leaves from sugar maples peppered the soggy ground as a chilly breeze moaned through the rushes of the swamp. A few hundred people, some of them Indians, gathered in a strange pilgrimage around a rough-hewn stone obelisk on an island in the middle of the swamp for some moments of meditation and solemn prayer—prayers of repentance, of remembrance, of brotherhood, and of death.

The occasion was American Indian Sunday; it comes traditionally the fourth Sunday in September—this pilgrimage into Rhode Island's Great Swamp. It marks the occasion of an event back in December 1675 when the greatest massacre in Rhode Island history occurred.

It's difficult to imagine this place as a place of bloodshed and violence, but on the high ground in the swamp are three cemeteries, and in one of them is the common grave of more than forty New Englanders killed by Indians during the early days of the colonies. The marker where people gather each September to commemorate the occasion is not at the site of the battle. The actual place where hundreds of men, women, and children—both Indians and whites—died is farther back in the swamp.

It happened just five days before Christmas in 1675. A column of more than a thousand men marched out of a snowy bivouac at Smith's Landing to attack the main stronghold of the Narragansett Indians who lived in the Great Swamp. For months, the colonies of Massachusetts Bay, Plymouth, and Connecticut had been at war with King Philip's Wampanoags, later assisted by Mipmucks and the Connecticut River Indians. The tribal warriors, numbering nearly 2,000, had been generally successful in a series of raids; thus the colonies were understandably concerned about their movements. When word was passed that the Narragansetts had joined King Philip's forces, the settlers felt it was time to move into battle.

The troops, in columns of two, consisted of 465 Massachusetts foot soldiers and 75 mounted on horseback, a Plymouth contingent of 158 infantry, and a Connecticut regiment of 315 foot soldiers, plus an auxiliary detachment of Mohegans and Pequots, invaluable as scouts. These made up a motley army, for they were not regulars in uniform. Instead, they were citizen soldiers in work clothes. Some wore helmets, but they would have looked more comfortable tilling the fields than marching into battle.

The firearms were a mixed lot, too. From many belts hung swords or hatchets. Thus armed and equipped, the colonials plodded doggedly through the snow, moving grimly toward their objective. At one o'clock they encountered enemy fire from Narragansett scouts, who rapidly fell back to the village, a veritable fortress that, had it not been for the frozen surface of the swamp, would have been difficult to approach. It actually occupied an island five or six acres in size and was contained with reinforced walls of stone and logs. But the colonials found a break in the barrier and made their assault on the fort.

Behind the walls of the Indian fortress stood the village, row upon row of bark wigwams, numbering into the hundreds. These were the homes of the Narragansetts,

1. *Pokeberries droop from the stalk in October; in other days, they would have been utilized by the Indians for making dye.*

2. *Gum, maple, and elm trees give color to the autumn landscape in the Great Swamp.*

1

2

even in winter. Had they not been taken by surprise they might have either taken their women and children into the swamp until the battle was over or met the approaching settlers at another place. But here all were subjected to the horrors of the battle. Not only were many of the Indians and settlers slain, but ultimately one of the wigwams caught fire, then another and another. Women and children screamed as their clothes were engulfed in flames. Snow began to fall from the darkening and ominous sky. The soldiers started to pull back into the swamp. They were not driven back, but they felt their job had been done. Besides, many of them were heartsick at the sounds of the women and children burning to death.

It required an all-night march to return to Smith's Landing, a grueling adventure since many of the citizen soldiers were wounded or sick. Some died along the way and were carried out of the swamp by their comrades. The Narragansetts buried the remainder and later requested a charge of gunpowder for each man they buried.

The war between the Narragansetts and the settlers was to continue for many months until King Philip and Canonchet, the Narragansett Indian chief, were both dead and their people and allies were dead, sold into slavery, or reduced to impotent remnants of the tribes they had once been.

The Great Swamp of Rhode Island, a 2,748-acre morass scooped out by an Ice Age glacier, bears remarkable contrast to the surrounding area, which supports one of the densest human populations in the United States.

While the swamp has played a role in local history, particularly during the Revolutionary War, it also is a place of wilderness which has changed little since the early days of this nation. A month prior to the Indian Day pilgrimage each year, the swamp swelters like an outdoor Turkish bath and the air is filled with the drone of mosquitoes and clouds of blackflies. Bloodthirsty horseflies, leeches, and no-see-ums make life miserable for the visitor. But at least there are no poisonous snakes, only the eastern water snake and a few blacksnakes, garter snakes, and other harmless varieties. Snapping turtles bask in the sun on the logs of half-submerged white cedar, and in the distance a lone osprey circles high above. Fifty years ago the bald eagle was occasionally spotted here.

One of the best times to see the swamp is during early autumn, after frost has dressed the trees in fall foliage. The many species of plant life then begin to take on more varied character (there are some 4,000 species of plant life here) and the bothersome insects have mostly disappeared. Trails and winding dirt roads lead through the thickest part of the swamp, where one may see rhododendron and dogwood growing close to sweet fern, trillium, bull briars, alders, maples, oaks, and even a jack-in-the-pulpit. Fall may be a bit late to see the latter; spring is a good time to see jack-in-the-pulpit, along with sweet-flowering pepperbush. In more open bogs are wild blueberries and mats of cranberries.

A boardwalk, built and maintained by the State Department of Natural Resources, which purchased the swamp in 1950 for just $23,400 as a wildlife management area, leads through a portion of the acreage. There are also

3. The bracket fungus, found in damp woods and swamps throughout much of the East.

4. Creeping jenny or ground cedar grows best in damp soil rarely inundated with water.

5. Turkey-tail fungus on a decaying log.

3

4

5

6. The cluster of mushrooms on top of the log are known Armillaria mellea, *autumn fungi which are parasites of numerous species of plants. Their color varies according to the species of plant or tree on which they grow. They are edible except after heavy rains or frost. The orange one is* Mycena galericalata, *also an edible species.*

6

7. *Lichen on a white oak tree.*

8. *Leaves settle in the autumn upon the dark-water pools of the swamp.*

9. *Hairy cup moss beginning to bloom (note blooms on tiny stems).*

10. *Bracket fungus.*

7

8

9

10

places where one can canoe, savoring the silent coves and interludes away from everything but the swamp itself. Some who enter the swamp hike along the railroad track leading along the western side, but the boardwalk offers the most rewarding opportunity for seeing wildlife and studying the varied botanical growth closeup.

As with the Corkscrew Sanctuary in southern Florida, the water level of the Great Swamp is maintained by a dike a mile long. Without it, a great deal of the area maintained as productive wildlife habitat would be dry indeed. And the swamp would be considerably less in size. But one is not generally aware of the efforts to keep the swamp as it appears. It is picturesque and primitive, lapping at the high ground called Great Neck, which many consider the most spectacular part of the reservation. From the water emerge countless islands, tussocks of waving grass, wood duck nests, and the whitened, ghostlike trunks of dead trees killed by the raised water level. Beyond the swamp lie farm fields and orchards which contrast dramatically with the wildness of this place.

Located virtually at the doorstep of the University of Rhode Island at nearby Kingston, the swamp is home for a multitude of wildlife, much of it unseen by the casual visitor. White-tailed deer are plentiful, and deer hunts are permitted in the autumn to slim down the herd for the winter months ahead when browse will be sparser. But in autumn also come other visitors—snow and Canada geese and a skyful of ducks migrating south. They settle mostly at Worden's Pond on the south edge of the swamp, and their calls add to the sounds of the area in autumn. Several families of Canada geese nest along the edge of the swamp, raising their young to join their cousins from the north on their southern migration.

Many of the students and faculty at the university utilize the swamp as an outdoor classroom or as a place of escape, for here one may find many places to be alone, places where man seemingly has had little impact through the years. The swamp is simply one of the finest examples of wilderness in this part of New England.

11

12

13

11. *Descendents of Indians and whites who once battled here gather at this monument each year in memory of those who lost their lives in the battle of the Great Swamp.*

12. *The vine with berries is known as greenbriar or bullbriar; the plant with tiny seed pods showing is sweet pepperbush, both common in the Great Swamp of Rhode Island.*

13. *Fireweed in the seeding stage following bloom in late summer.*

14. *The New York aster blooms in the early autumn or late summer.*

CHAPTER
5
Four Holes Swamp

Man did his first wondering in wilderness with an innocent mind, having no past to trouble him and no answers. The world was new and fresh to him then and full of magic . . . We do our wondering differently now. Our world is older, with too much of its magic gone.

—Peggy Wayburn

From the sea, warm breezes usher in the scent of spring past the salt-water marshes to South Carolina's low country. The warmth of an April sun filters dimly through the thick green canopy of great bald cypress, sweet gum, and tupelo, many of them old when America was discovered, to the liquid black-water floor of Four Holes Swamp.

Tree frogs trill, bullfrogs grunt, a prothonotary warbler sings from a secluded perch covered by the overgrowth. From beyond the great tapered columns of the cypress, the hunting horn call of a pileated woodpecker echoes through the aisles of black water, filling the vaulted spaces and rooms of the swamp until once again a primeval silence settles. The water rustles against a downed twig, and then the creatures of the swamp begin their symphony all over again to signal the drama of new life in the spring.

The Four Holes lingers in the memory. Some say it is the most impressive swamp in all of America. Here lies an 1,800-acre tract of virgin cypress. It is all the things one would expect a swamp to be—like an artist's rendition.

Scientists come from many parts of the nation to study the Four Holes, for it is such an excellent example of a black-water swamp; i.e., simply a swamp characterized by its black water. Charles H. Wharton, professor of biology at Georgia State University and author of *The Southern River Swamp,* describes the Four Holes as a "jewel ecosystem." He defines ecosystem as a unit of environment which has a structure, such as a characteristic routing of minerals or water. The Four Holes, in other words, presents a well-defined total swamp.

Barely saved from the clutches of men who would cut the timber and drain the swamp, Four Holes was purchased in 1971 by The Nature Conservancy and the National Audubon Society to be preserved as a sanctuary. Located just thirty-five miles northwest of Charleston between the towns of Holly Hill and Harleyville, the sanctuary contains 3,415 acres. It is bounded on two sides by high bluffs and elsewhere by cut-over swamp, thus forming a rectangle some five miles long and up to one-and-a-half-miles wide in some places. The sanctuary is by no means all of the swamp, which stretches some sixty-five miles and is in fact a tributary of the Edisto River.

In 1969 parts of what is today the sanctuary were cut over, and it was that action, more than any other, which moved those who knew and loved the swamp to seek support for saving it.

The swamp at that time belonged to the Francis Beidler family of Chicago, timber magnates since the turn of this century with holdings in various parts of the nation including South Carolina. The Beidler family once operated the Santee River Cypress Lumber Co., which carried out extensive timbering operations in the general area. At this writing, they still hold the major uncut portion of the Congaree Swamp just outside Columbia, which conservationists hope somehow to preserve as a national park.

Robert Knoth of Charleston, consulting forester and representative of the Beidlers in South Carolina, helpfully provided maps and timber cruise data to the Nature Conservancy and to Audubon during their campaign to save the swamp. Nonetheless, it was no easy matter to raise $1,450,000, the agreed-upon price of the sanctuary area.

A number of money-making schemes were put into effect.

The Columbia chapter of the Audubon Society staged a sale of pileated woodpecker prints by artist Anne Richardson of Charleston and donated the profits toward the purchase of Four Holes. "We knew this wouldn't buy very much land," explained Audubon chapter president Bill Campbell, "but we wanted to do whatever we could to help out . . . besides, it gave people who didn't have a lot of money to spend the opportunity to contribute something toward the swamp."

The purchase of the swamp practically drained the Audubon coffer and left few funds for any development such as boardwalks, a nature center, or educational programs. A two-man staff was employed and canoe trails marked. Nonetheless, Peter Manigault, publisher of the *Charleston News & Courier* and then a member of the board of directors of the National Audubon Society, and others were proud that it could be done. "You cannot set a definitive value upon such places," Manigault said. "Once you visit the Four Holes, you know this place is beyond any price that can be placed upon it, whether it be in dollars, lira, or yen."

From the exterior, Four Holes appears to be an impenetrable jungle. But once inside—and the best way to enter is via the main canoe trail—the swamp opens up into a kind of natural cathedral. The interior is uncluttered and spacious, with the clean-boled cypresses rising out of sight through a secondary canopy spread by massive, buttressed gum trees.

The threat of rain permeated the air as Doug Clayton, field technician for Audubon at Four Holes, and I launched our seventeen-foot aluminum canoe and paddled across a small lake to an opening in the green curtain. Beyond those portals lay a world of another dimension—a paradise lost and found again. The great trees allowed only an occasional glimpse at the skies. Around the base some of these giants were more than fifteen feet in circumference.

We glided silently through the dark, mirrored waterways, carefully picking out marker after marker lest we take a wrong turn.

"I've been lost several times in this swamp," my guide confided. "And sometimes I didn't think I was going to find my way out again." Doug Clayton was born only a couple of miles down the road from the swamp and spent more time in the Four Holes than he spent on the family farm. "It's been a mecca to me ever since I learned of its existence," he said. "I used to come in here to hunt deer, but that was before the sanctuary was established. Now all I want to do is come here and experience it time after time. You can never get enough of this place."

The canoe skimmed along silently and swiftly, even though we were pushing against a slow current that carried an occasional leaf or bright red smilax berry past us. A sudden thunder of wings overhead interrupted the serenity as a great barred owl, startled from its high perch, disappeared through the trees to find another spot of seclusion. Later in the day, we heard it calling and another answering from far away across the swamp.

Two or three times during the day, rain misted through

1

the canopy. We could see it almost like fog drifting down, and it all but dissipated before reaching the swamp floor. At one point, the sun escaped from behind the storm clouds to cast a rainbow down through the roof of the swamp.

Giant logs felled by time lay covered in fluorescent moss along the waterways. They were clasped between clusters of colossal cypress knees, crowned here and there with spreading clumps of poison ivy. The logs made sundecks for the swamp's cold-blooded creatures, and atop many of them were either cottonmouth moccasins, their yellow-blotched scales dull from the winter's aging, or the great brown water snake, a big rough-scaled snake often mistaken by the layman for the poisonous variety.

Once that day we came suddenly upon a small family of otter, playfully chasing one another around a cluster of cypress knees, but when they spotted us they disappeared. A minute later, we glimpsed one of them surfacing for air a good fifty feet away, but that was the last we saw of them. Otter live throughout the swamp, but are among the shyest animals in the Four Holes.

Although the swamp gives the immediate impression that there is virtually no understory, more than 120 species of woody plants were counted in the area by John Dennis, a botanist and ornithologist working with the Nature Conservancy. Among them is the green-fly orchid, its petaled blooms picturesquely spread on the limbs of hardwoods throughout the swamp. Resurrection ferns and cardinal flowers grow along the main streams and add a rare beauty dating back to Pleistocene times.

As we glided along, sometimes poling our way over logs and debris that cluttered the canoe trail, a steady chorus of unseen songbirds kept us company—among them Carolina wrens, blue-gray gnatcatchers, and prothonotary warblers. The Four Holes, some say, is still home to the ivory-billed woodpecker. More professional opinions discount that probability, but it may well harbor the rare Bachman's warbler.

Most large wading birds are fish eaters and depend upon keen vision to catch their prey on sight. For this reason, the great herons and egrets are rare visitors to the Four Holes. The giant trees shut out most of the daylight, and this, combined with the currents, high water levels, and dark water color, makes the fish nearly invisible. Although the birds can't see them well, there are fish inhabiting these waters—mainly the Chologaster or rice-field fish, ancestor of the blind cave fish similar to those found in the underground streams at Mammoth Cave National Park; stumpknockers, largemouth bass, and red breasts or bream. There are also great crayfish and gar, which are a mainstay of the alligator's diet.

The Four Holes has played an extensive role in the history of the area. It may have been the last sanctuary of the Natchez Indians of South Carolina. Entries in the Journal of Commons show that the Colonial House of Commons decided on September 16, 1733, that the Natchez Indians "now encamped at Four Holes Swamp be sent as soon as possible to scout about Port Royal." Later, the Natchez were placed on an island reservation in Port Royal Sound. Pieces of Indian pottery, arrowheads,

1. Moss grows upon moss in this moisture-laden land; during winter, deer browse upon it.

2. The brown water snake has a more vicious disposition than the cottonmouth, but its bite is nontoxic. This one basks on a log amid verdant vines of poison ivy.

2

3. One of the four holes which give the swamp its name.

and other artifacts, are still occasionally uncovered in the sandy loam fields adjacent to the swamp.

The Four Holes, early in the American Revolution, was a hideout for the Swamp Fox—Gen. Francis Marion—and his guerrillas. It was an excellent base for their forays upon the British regulars. They could strike quickly and literally disappear into what the British considered a terrifying place, filled with poisonous snakes and man-eating alligators. It would have been easy for the swamp to swallow up an entire company of soldiers.

The braided waterways twist and turn, sometimes so sharply it's necessary to take some of the rights or lefts in double hitches. If you miss the markers on the canoe trail, you probably won't get very far, for the waterway closes in on you, forcing you to back your craft to the point of departure. And yet as you stand off and look at it from any vantage point, the swamp appears an endless array of free-form rooms and corridors under a ceiling of glowing submarine green not duplicated anywhere else on earth.

Periodically we came upon one of the lakes—the natives call them holes—where the forest broke away, letting the sunlight through to glimmer upon the dark waters. There are reportedly four such lakes or holes within the swamp, and it's from these that some people claim the swamp took its name—Four Holes.

In fact, one source of the swamp waters may lie in those deep holes where gators foray by night and sunbathe by day. While there is drainage water coming down from the sandhills, much of the lifeblood is provided by subterranean springs. And while there are mainstreams of flow toward the Edisto and the sea, they are not easily detected early in the spring when the waters are high, and sometimes only with much searching at other times of the year. For the swamp, even when other areas nearby are dried by severe drought, never seems to suffer for lack of water.

Norman Brunswig, superintendent of Four Holes Sanctuary, says he likes to think of the swamp as an ego experience. "You can be feeling low," he explained, "and go into the swamp. Soon you feel a regeneration of spirit and the confidence that all goes well once again."

4

5

6

7

8

4. *Huge cypress knees such as these emerging from the tree roots restrict movement by canoe through the swamp.*

5. *Butterweed, which grows profusely in the higher elevations of the swamp, brilliantly colors the landscape from March to May.*

6. *The poisonous cottonmouth moccasin, sometimes referred to as the keeper of the swamp, spends long hours sunning, but normally catches its food in the water.*

7. *The black water is occasionally broken by patches of fern.*

8. *The common names of many plants came about merely because of their resemblance to something else. The sword fern, which often grows in decaying wood or logs, is no exception.*

CHAPTER

6

The Okefenokee

Standing here in the deep, brooding silence all the wilderness seems motionless, as if the work of creation were done. But in the midst of this . . . we know there is incessant motion and change.

—John Muir

The swamp, cloaked in a shroud of fog, is ominously silent. Gaunt cypress trees, their limbs draped with strands of Spanish moss, and clumps of bay bushes become imaginary creatures of a prehistoric era. Except for the occasional splash of a fish somewhere in this gray void, only the methodical swish of the canoe paddle tethers the visitor to reality.

Fading into the mist on every side are watery prairies spiked with golden club or never-wet lily pads, their virgin white flowers half-closed, waiting for the morning sun to open fully.

The Okefenokee is the water dome of southeastern Georgia, an artesian teacup that forever overflows. Although the movement of water is imperceptible, the swamp is in fact the headwater for two rivers—the St. Marys, flowing southeast through Florida to the Atlantic Ocean, and the Suwannee which drifts southwestward through Florida to the Gulf of Mexico.

The sources of the Okefenokee's water remains somewhat a mystery, for the swamp, unlike virtually any other swamp in America, is higher than its surrounding territory. There's no hard evidence of artesian supplies, either, or even percolation. Some say the major source is simply rain-water. The Okefenokee has may faces—open watery prairies, lakes with clear water that harbor large-mouth bass and a fish sometimes called the Okefenokee's "shark"—the jack pickerel. There are cathedral stands of tall cypress protecting the open waterways with a canopy so dense the sunlight seldom penetrates. It is sprinkled with islands and islands-to-be—floating masses of matted roots on which major life forms have begun to take shape. These islands gave rise to the name Okefenokee which means "Land of the Trembling Earth."

The Okefenokee is forever changing, building up, tearing down, bringing together. Here the forces of nature, subtle as they may seem, actually create new land. All over the prairie portions of the swamp are floating patches of peat, the result of the constant, hidden work of plant life. They represent one of the many stages of its eventual consolidation into something approaching dry land. Plant generations follow each other with such rapidity that the cycle of life, death, and decay—the process of rendering living matter back into chemical biota—goes on continuously. Gas, formed in quantity by the decay of sunken, dead vegetation and trapped under the peat, gathers so thickly it lifts an entire chunk of the bottom material to the surface and keeps it afloat. Aptly, the swampers dub this phenomenon a blow-up. The larger ones are called batteries, some measuring twenty-five feet wide and more than a hundred feet long. Once the newly exposed material floats to the surface, it accepts seeds sown by the winds, by birds, and by other creatures of the swamp.

As the smaller life forms grow—tiny grasses and aquatic weeds—larger ones, such as bayberry and elder, take hold, extending roots downward into the water until they reach the peat bottom. There they anchor themselves and their floating islands to the swamp. But it may be many years before the mass becomes solid, before there is no more water passing under it.

Periodically severe fires have plagued the swamp, but

1. *A low aerial view of the Okefenokee as seen from the observation tower at Okefenokee Swamp Park near Waycross.*

2. *An aerial view of Chesser Prairie shows an ample sprinkling of tree islands.*

3. *Bonnet lilies on an Okefenokee waterway.*

4. *Along the Fargo side of the Okefenokee are vast stands of cypress such as this.*

1

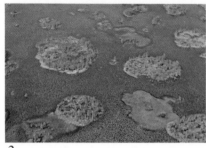

2

3

they are considered a part of the natural cycle. Usually the result of lightning during extensive drought periods, these fires are said to be responsible for the Okefenokee's great prairies or marshland, which total some 60,000 acres. Surface layers of peat were burned so low that woody plants could not grow back. Recent fires swept parts of the Okefenokee in 1932, and again in 1954–55 the peat base along the western edge of the swamp was burned deeply. When the swamp refilled with water, these deep burns eroded, and the flow of the Suwannee River increased to the point where it threatened to drain the swamp. To hold back the water, a five-mile sill was constructed in 1960 from Mack's Island to Pine Island. This ridge of sand holds back the water, and a deep channel with a sandy bottom lies in back of it. In March largemouth bass from the western part of the swamp migrate here to spawn.

Aside from the canoe and boat trails which cross the swamp in a dozen different places, the Okefenokee is a massive lake with varied vegetation. Except for several open bodies of water and gator holes, one can walk throughout most of the swamp, for the peat bottom offers fairly firm footing. Virtually no one explores the swamp on foot, however. Instead the swamp attracts canoeists by the thousands each year, mostly during the fall, winter, and spring months. During that time, the insects are bearable. In the summer, clouds of mosquitoes discourage most visitors. Also, the heat and humidity during the months of May through September are oppressive.

Prairies in the eastern section provide a major year-round habitat of the Florida sandhill crane, a threatened species. Some seventy pine-clad islands occupy another 25,000 acres and the remainder of the swamp fluctuates between solid and liquid with the exception of the open water lakes, which account for a considerable area. In fact, there are sixty of them large enough to be named scattered throughout the swamp.

This peat-filled swamp traces its history to the Pleistocene era, when the Atlantic Ocean came inland about seventy-five miles beyond its present coast. When the ocean receded and the land here rose to its present 110 to 130 feet above sea level, rains ultimately washed out the salt water and the swamp became a fresh-water lake. Had the water been deep, it likely would still be a fresh-water lake; but instead it was shallow—often no more than two feet deep—and with the buildup over the years of additional peat, it has become even more shallow, and gradually the lake became vegetated.

The slow-running water of the Okefenokee is held in a shallow basin of sand and impeded by congregations of cypress, by vast areas of sphagnum moss, by dense thickets of shrubs, and by islands thronged with pines. From its northernmost reaches in Georgia some forty miles north of the Florida border, the swamp flows generally south about twenty miles until the moving water reaches roughly the midpoint of the Okefenokee. There, approximately at Billy's Island, a branch turns west and heads for the Suwannee River exit. Then, at a point some fifteen miles southwest of Billy's Island, another branch begins to flow through a stream that eventually becomes the St. Marys River.

5. *A swallowtail butterfly.*

6. *Tree frogs often are found clinging to stubble or bushes a foot above the waterline.*

7. *A damselfly, cousin to the dragonfly, rests on a lily pad.*

8. *The flowering water lily has become almost a trademark of the*

5

6

7

8

Okefenokee. The best time to see them is in May when the prairies are literally covered with blossoms.

9. *Blooms of Virginia sweet spire resemble willow catkins, but are lighter and whiter.*

10. *A garter snake probes its way among the branches of a loblolly bay tree.*

11. *Drops of water —the vital element of any swamp—cling to vines following a spring shower.*

9

10

12. *Wild iris bloom profusely in the Okefenokee in April.*

13. *Pitcher plants, more commonly found in damp soil without standing water, find conditions tolerable in the Okefenokee.*

14. *A close-up of the green carpet provided by sphagnum moss.*

15. *(Overleaf) The Okefenokee is noted for its marvelous reflections.*

11

12

13

14

16

17

Of all the various habitats, the largest and most densely forested has been staked out by the cypress trees. The most extensive of these areas—twenty or more acres—are called bays, a misnomer perhaps borrowed from wooded swamps in Florida where bay trees flourish. Sunlight nourishes a dense flowering underbrush at the fringes of these cypress concentrations, but seldom reaches inside them. It is here, inside this curtain of jungle, that the swamp justifies its reputation as a place of deep and mysterious gloom. It is here, too, that much of the wildlife is found.

Perhaps these places of gloom first attracted the American Indian. Initially the swamp was the hunting ground for several tribes, and their burial mounds dot the numerous islands in the swamp to this day. Later, the Okefenokee became a place of refuge for renegade Indians who came to be known as Seminoles, an offspring of the Creek nation. From their island homes deep within the swamp, they made raids against both the Creeks and the first white settlers in the area, sometimes slaughtering entire families and returning to the swamp with their scalps. By 1838 the problem became so critical that orders were issued for troops to clear the swamplands of the Indians.

Many of those who lived in the vicinity believed the task to be an impossibility. Little was actually known of how large the swamp was, what dangers lay within its realms. It was largely unexplored, and no one had a great desire to find out. But a detachment of troops under the leadership of Gen. Charles Floyd was formed at Fort Gilmer which stood near what is today Fargo. These troops marched into the swamp, following the Indian trails through quaking bogs and along watery terrain. When they arrived at the Indian village, they found it abandoned. The Indians had already learned of their coming and had disappeared into the surrounding swamp. Rather than chance tracking the Indians down in such unfamiliar territory, the troops burned the village and marched on to the eastern boundary of the swamp.

While they didn't get the Indians, their action was enough to discourage any further attacks, and soon thereafter the Seminoles moved south to the Florida Everglades and the Big Cypress Swamp which has been their home ever since.

The Indian problem was resolved, but the Okefenokee's real troubles were just beginning. With the Indians gone, the white man began to assess the economic value of the swamp. It possessed great timber assets, and the rich black peat base might, if the swamp were drained, provide some of the best farmland in America. Negotiations were launched with the state of Georgia, and in 1889 a portion of the swamp was sold to a private corporation whose purpose was to drain the rich muckland for agricultural development. An Atlanta man, Capt. Harry Jackson, assembled a crew on the eastern periphery of the swamp near what is now the community of Folkston in 1891, where he started construction of the Suwannee Canal. The canal would not only serve to drain the swamp, but it could also be used to float out the valuable cypress timber harvested. With ox and mule, the workers dredged the canal some fourteen miles into the swamp from Camp Cornelia, but things didn't go exactly as planned.

The farther the canal diggers dug, the more hopeless the entire plan appeared to be. For instead of draining the water out of the swamp, the canal brought more water in from outside. With a high underground water table, the big ditch tapped into it and started water flowing west into the Okefenokee. After millions of dollars of work and study had gone into the project, it finally was abandoned and later became known as Jackson's Folly. The Suwannee Canal has stood all these years as a monument to man's failure in another of his attempts to conquer the swamp. It remains the principal point of entry to the U.S. Fish and Wildlife's portion of the Okefenokee.

As a result of the canal fiasco, people were now more fully acquainted with Okefenokee; and with the Indians gone, more and more men poled their boats into the swamp in search of game. Bear, deer, cougar, and alligator were plentiful. The swamp's fur-bearing animals were in demand, and so were alligator hides. Hunting and trapping became a profitable profession. And the timber was still there.

The big push into the swamp by timber interests began in earnest in 1908 when the Hebard Cypress Company moved in. They constructed tram roads into the swamp from their mill at Waycross, and loggers removed millions of board feet of top-grade cypress on those trams. The giant pine stands on Billy's Island and the cypress trees of Jackson's Bay were leveled. It began to appear that regardless of the failure of the Suwannee Canal to drain the swamp, the Okefenokee was still in deep trouble. Narrow-gauge railroad lines supported by miles of spindly pilings reached like skeleton fingers into the very heart of the swamp, and a large logging mill was ultimately located on Billy's Island.

With people coming and going each day, with the ring of the lumberjack's ax and the sound of his saw penetrating the swamp, the wildlife retreated to the innermost sanctums of the wilderness. Still they were not safe. The hunters and trappers were everywhere.

The effort to save the Okefenokee began with the formation in 1918 of a small group in Waycross which called itself the Okefenokee Preservation Society. The purpose of the society would be "to give authentic publicity regarding the Okefenokee Swamp and somehow secure its reservation and preservation for public, educational, scientific and recreational uses."

Pressure was soon brought to bear on political factions, and in 1919 the Georgia Legislature passed a resolution calling on the federal government to purchase the Okefenokee in order to preserve it from destruction. Nothing more happened until 1926, when two local men—Alex McQueen of Folkston and Hamp Mizell, who had lived a good part of his life in the swamp—published a book called *History of the Okefenokee Swamp*. That started a flurry of newspaper feature articles about this never-never land, and the swamp's qualities as a wildlife sanctuary were recognized.

In 1931 the U.S. Senate sent a special committee on Conservation of Wildlife Resources to the swamp, and in

16. *A common egret perched atop a bay tree in the Okefenokee Swamp.*

17. *Baby egrets in their nest.*

18. *The Florida sandhill crane, a threatened species, nests in the Okefenokee Swamp, hatching its young in April or early May.*

19. *The black vulture plays an important ecological role in any swamp; here a tree full of them dry off from the night's dewfall before finding a thermal on which to soar above the swamp.*

18

19

20. *(Overleaf) In early spring, some of the watery prairies of the Okefenokee are covered with gardens of carnivorous bladderwort, which devour insects.*

(Wendell Metzen photo).

65

21. *A close-up view of the carnivorous sundew plant.*

22. *Lady's hatpins are scattered throughout the prairie portions of the Okefenokee.*

23. *Tickseed, which resembles the sneezeweed in color, blooms from June to August.*

23

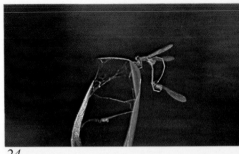

24

21

22

25

24. *Mating dragonflies.*

25. *Part of the flower garden that is the Okefenokee is golden club, sometimes locally called never-wet. Because of a protective coating, the leaves shed water without becoming wet.*

26. *A chameleon making its way down the trunk of a small tree blends with the colors of the bay leaves.*

26

27. *Sprays of arrowhead are framed by the reflections of cypress trees.*

28. *Sneezeweed, sometimes called the swamp sunflower, grows from two to six feet high. Normally it flowers from August to October.*

29. *Some feel that marsh pinks are among the most beautiful of all the Okefenokee's wildflowers.*

27

29

28

30. *(Overleaf) Cypress trees during low water show their vast buttresses.*

(Wendell Metzen photo).

31

32

33

34

31. *A single alligator egg. The young gator, when ready to hatch, uses a pointed "egg-tooth" to break his way out of the shell.*

32. *A young gator emerges from the egg.*

33. *If the carnivorous pitcher plant in the foreground has any notions of devouring this twelve-foot Okefenokee alligator, it had better think again. A close look into the mouth of this giant gator will reveal the teeth, worn down to the*

roots by use. Gators live to be fifty to sixty years of age, and this one may be nearly that old.

34. *While alligators mostly feed at night and spend their days lying in the sun on embankments such as this one, there are no set rules. You may find one searching for food during midday.*

35. *The alligator likes to remain as inconspicuous as possible. Here one hides himself in a clump of grass. Although they appear*

clumsy, the gator can actually exceed a horse in speed—during the first fifteen feet of his sprint. This is largely due to the catapult effect he accomplishes with his tail.

36. *Young gators have black and yellow striped colorations until they are more than a year old.*

35

36

1937 the Okefenokee National Wildlife Refuge was established.

From that day forward, the swamp began to recover. With heavy rainfall, hot sun, and rich underlying soil, the plant growth soon covered many of the scars left by man. The wildlife began to move back into all portions of the swamp. Not all problems were solved, however. The Okefenokee is a big place. Now that the federal government had established a wildlife refuge, no game could be shot. Many of the hunters resented this limitation on their freedom, and they continued hunting as they had done all along. They were violating the law now, so they had to be sneaky about it. Most of the hunting was done at night. The main prey was the alligator, and poaching gators in the Okefenokee was to remain very much a problem for many years to come. Only when the sale of products made from gator hides became unlawful in the 1970s was the poaching virtually eliminated.

When Congress designated the Okefenokee an official wilderness in 1974, it took one further step to insure the swamp's protection. In that bill, 353,981 of the 435,000 acres in the swamp were established as the Okefenokee Wilderness, which puts limitations on its use. Even air space must not be violated below 2,000 feet altitude.

In addition to the national wildlife refuge portion of the Okefenokee, there are also the Okefenokee Swamp Park, a private enterprise leasing a portion of the swamp near the northern perimeter just seven miles out of Waycross, Ga., and the Stephen Foster State Park, located on the southwestern side. The two parks and an access point at the Suwannee River Canal in the wildlife refuge offer the only three access points to this swamp measuring some twenty-five miles across at its widest point.

Despite the fact that canoe trails range through most of the swamp today, it remains a place of brooding atmosphere and mysterious beauty, a place that has changed remarkably little since early pioneers first became acquainted with it.

The Congaree

Through all the wonderful,
eventful centuries . . . God has cared for these trees,
saved them from drought, disease, avalanches and
a thousand straining, leveling tempests and floods;
but he cannot save them from fools . . .

—John Muir

Most people believe the age of giants existed only in fairy tales, but in a broad expanse of red-river bottomland less than thirty minutes' drive toward the sea from South Carolina's capital city you can still find giants, towering more than 125 feet above the floodplain of the Congaree River. They call this place the Congaree Swamp.

The giants are trees—many of them state record holders, some of them national champions. And while none represent the remains of an endangered species, with the possible exception of the bald cypress, they are all, in a sense, endangered. For at no other place in all of eastern America can one find a greater collection of giant trees in one place than in the Congaree Swamp. So precious are they that in 1974 a Congaree Swamp National Preserve Association was formed with the objective of preserving 70,000 acres as part of the national park system. It would be similar in management and status to the Big Thicket National Preserve in Texas, so designated by Congress in 1974.

Although the Congaree is not without reminders of man—it is flooded periodically by the river which flows through Columbia, a sizable city, and deposits its debris including plastic containers, beer and soft drink cans, broken styrofoam picnic coolers, and glass bottles—it has an atmosphere of a veritable wilderness. There's generally little understory throughout the 70,000-plus-acre swamp to distract one's attention from the tree-giants. One can walk here alone and be dwarfed by living things which put the life-style of man in proper perspective.

While some of the Congaree cypress had already fallen before the ax and saw of the lumberjack prior to 1975, some 11,000 acres of forest are now as they must have appeared before the European discovery of America. Scattered throughout the tract are trees that have spanned centuries—bald cypress with trunk circumferences of up to twenty-five feet, sweet gum, water tupelo, loblolly pine, cottonwood, oak, hickory, many so large they beggar description.

The bases of sweet gum trees found in the Congaree exceed 15 feet in circumference; southern red oak, 18 feet; swamp white oak, 14 feet; willow oak, 13 feet. But particularly significant are the loblolly pines, which normally do not exist in a climax forest such as this one. Here, however, some calculated to be more than 300 years old tower as high as 160 feet and measure 15 feet or more around their bases; their bark appears more as armor than the woody substance of a tree. Normally in such a mature forest, hardwoods tend to crowd out the pines. But here hardwoods and pines have been growing side by side for hundreds of years without either yielding to the competition. The pines consistently thrive, growing larger than anywhere else in the east.

Scientists who have studied the matter believe the pines achieved their start among the hardwoods during some type of natural disturbance such as disease or hurricanes and survived merely because they managed to outgrow the surrounding hardwoods.

Ornithologist John V. Dennis, who has spent much time in the Congaree over some thirty years, puts forth one possible explanation for the loblolly's presence in the

Congaree. Dennis suggests that during a series of drought years the swamp became dry enough to have caught fire. Remains of ancient charred stumps in some higher areas support this theory. A tremendous conflagration may have opened up parts of the swamp enough to allow seeding by loblolly pines and room for good growth. Dennis says this may have happened several times during the past few hundred years, since there appears to be more than one age group represented among the pines. Some are around 180 years old, for instance; others around 300 years old. Charlotte Green, in her book *Trees of the South*, mentions a severe drought—determined by rings on an ancient cypress tree—that occurred around 1786. This drought, said Dennis, coincides with one age group of the Congaree pines.

Whatever the cause, there appears to have been an interruption of the normal development of the climax forest here. It remains somewhat a mystery.

The Congaree is a typical example of a red-river-bottom swamp—red because that is the color of the silt carried down and deposited during the flood stage of the stream from the South Carolina hills and the Piedmont plateau. The swamp depends upon the river for its existence, for without the periodic flooding, it would cease to be swamp altogether. Although it occupies both sides of the river which meanders lazily toward the sea from Columbia, most of the giant trees are located on the north side of the stream, and that is the portion conservation groups are interested in saving for posterity.

Interlaced with slow-moving meandering streams, sloughs or guts, as they are locally called, and marshes, the Congaree Swamp extends to the river's confluence with the Wateree and then is lost in another swamp—the Santee, which already has come under state protection. The Congaree Swamp may be inundated by floodwaters from the river at all seasons of the year without pattern or regularity. But the waters soon withdraw, and the swamp dries out to a great extent, so that it is usually negotiable, especially in autumn. In this way, it plays a major part in the ecosystem of this area. For as the river begins to flood, the flow in the streams and sloughs is reversed. Water, laden with fertile agricultural soils from farms upstream from Columbia, begins flowing back into the swamp, spilling into depressions which act as reservoirs. Not only does water fill every gut, pond, and oxbow lake, but large quantities are absorbed by the root systems of the giant trees and by the clay-base soil itself.

The flooding does no damage to the trees, for most of the species found in lower elevations here—cypress, water elm, poplar, tupelo gum, buttonbush, and ash—can live year-round partially inundated by water. In fact, they grow best in standing water, but cypress and many other moisture-loving plants require a period when the soil is free of standing water in order for them to propagate. The oaks, hickories, sweet gum, sycamore, sugarberry, and cottonwood grow at slightly higher elevations in the swamp.

As the river flood begins to correct itself, conditions are again reversed in the swamp. And the floodwaters, minus much fertile silt, are again poured back into the river. The

1

4

1. *Many of the great trees of the Congaree are among the largest found in the east. This pine stands nearly 125 feet tall.*

2. *Huge muscadine grapevines grow to the treetops, but produce little fruit. Here sap from a vine jelled with bacteria indicates where a sapsucker tapped the vine a few days previously.*

3. *Red polybore fungus is but one of several kinds of fungi in the Congaree. It grows on dead trees.*

4. *The Congaree in flood offers a display of shadows upon the muddy waters.*

2

3

George Taylor

5. *Swamp buttercup is one of the predominant wildflowers in spring bloom.*

6. *Wild azalea, which grows along the edge of the Congaree, lends breathtaking beauty in the spring, usually blooming in April and May.*

7. *These lilylike flowers are known locally as ''naked ladies.'' Blooming in March and April, usually in heavily wooded areas, the bulbs were once used by the Seminole Indians to cure toothaches. Their range is from South Carolina to Florida.*

8. *The sulphur butterfly gathers nectar from the cardinal flower. Various species of the sulphur butterfly are found from southern Indiana into South America.*

9. *Following the traditional spring floods, the floor of the Congaree becomes a garden of wildflowers, sedges, mosses, and grass.*

5

6

7

8

9

swamp, in a sense, has acted as a cleansing agent, taking particles from the water and returning it to the stream in a purer state. Yet it is these particles which help the great trees to grow and to thrive. Without these nutrients, the great trees would never have achieved such size.

Most of the lands on which the great trees stand belong to the Francis Beidler family of Chicago, great timber magnates since long before the turn of the century. Much of the Beidler tract had been leased to various hunt clubs, which, following campaigns by conservationists to have the area set aside as a national park, promptly erected "No Trespassing" signs.

There are mounds in the Congaree that are believed to be manmade. Once moonshine stills for making illegal whiskey were supposedly located on them. But they were also used for places of refuge for livestock during time of flood. Reputedly built by slave labor, some mounds were no more than two to three feet above the rest of the swamp floor, but at times that was sufficient for cattle to survive a flood. John Dennis says he once measured a cattle mound in the Congaree that was 100 feet long, 50 feet wide, and 6 to 7 feet high, one of the larger ones known. He added that their age was confirmed through trees growing atop them which were more than 125 years old.

More than once politicians and others have expressed the desire to make Columbia a seaport, to either channel the Congaree River or build an adjacent canal which would permit navigation of huge barges and boats from the sea to this inland city. In so doing, it would tap the supply of water for the Congaree Swamp, and in its place would be only devastation. Harry Hampton, longtime columnist for the Columbia *State* newspaper and one of the most outspoken conservationists of South Carolina, calls it an outrageous idea that would be extremely costly and might not even work anyway. The idea is not likely, many feel, to become a reality, but stranger projects have come to pass in other swamps.

In 1963 the National Park Service published results of an extensive study it conducted on the Congaree and recommended it become a 21,000-acre national monument. Said the Park Service: "The conclusions of this survey were that a biological community of rare quality and considerable scientific value exists. Since that time when the survey was completed, there have been investigations by Park Service personnel of other similar areas in the southeast, but none was found which appeared to contain geological and biological significance comparable to the Congaree Swamp." Nowhere else were such varieties of giant trees found.

Dr. Charles H. Wharton, biologist at Georgia State University, wrote in *The Southern River Swamps*: "The river swamps are ideal examples of what we mean by 'open space,' 'green belts,' and 'natural corridors.' They may function in many ways: sponges for regulation of vital water cycle, giant kidneys for waste purification, convalescent wards for the esthetically ill, outdoor classrooms for school children and oxygen machines for air quality."

The Congaree represents all these things, and its future is still very much in doubt.

10. A species of grapevine found here has aerial roots dangling from the vines which eventually will reach the ground and penetrate it.

11. A lone brown water snake seeks out a spot to warm in the sun on the debris-littered floor of the Congaree.

12. A wild turkey

11

Billy Durant / South Carolina Wildlife

12

CHAPTER
8
Woods Bay

The equation of man and earth ought to be
more comprehensive, and understood in more senses
than those used by science and industrial utility.
We talk ecology, but we have scarcely taken
the first step toward applying it.

—John Hay

A narrow, sand-paved country road filled with watery potholes and marginal ruts leads off South Carolina Highway 152 past farmland bounded by flimsy woven-wire fences. Soon the pasture fields disappear into low scrub, slash pine, and oak, and the roadbed scrambles up a low ridge of soft white sand. On the east, this marks the perimeter of Woods Bay, one of the genuine mysteries in the world of nature.

Located in Sumter and Clarendon counties three miles from the tiny town of Olanta, S.C., Woods Bay is but one of several thousand so-called Carolina Bays which sprinkle the Atlantic Coastal Plain from North Carolina through parts of Georgia. They have been studied by many geologists, but rarely do any two experts agree upon how the bays, most of them swampy morasses filled with dense populations of wildlife, were actually born. Some claim they were created by a meteorite shower; others believe it was subterranean pressures.

Other theories foster the idea that the bays were formed by artesian water flows which washed out the sands; or that the bays are leftovers from swirling schools of fish stranded by the receding ocean when this area was indeed covered by an ancient sea. Richard Porcher, Jr., a Citadel University botany professor, subscribes to a different theory. He believes the Carolina Bays were formed by a sump action. It is a complicated theory, but Porcher says it makes the most sense, all factors considered.

The sand ridge borders much of Woods Bay—as it does many of the other Carolina Bays. According to one theory, this sand was bulldozed up by exploding meteorites which showered the coastal plain as much as 40,000 years ago. Beyond the dry sand ridge, the swamp begins abruptly. On the east, the scrub trees give way to watery prairies of marsh grasses. Clumps of titi and bay, punctuated with sparse growths of young pond cypress, are scattered throughout the marsh, which covers some 500 acres of the 1500-acre total area of Woods Bay. Eventually, botanists believe, the marsh will give way to forest—pond cypress, tupelo gum, green ash, and, ultimately, bald cypress. It may take centuries, they concede, before that is accomplished.

The border between marsh and woodland is almost as abrupt as the boundaries of the swamp itself. Pond cypress and sweet gum crowd out into the prairie of water lilies and marsh grasses. And then, appearing suddenly among them, are the giant tupelo gum and bald cypress. Farther into the forested portions, the sun is obscured by a dense canopy decorated with long strands of Spanish moss. From the watery floor of the swamp spring clumps of royal fern and arrowhead.

Although most of the marsh section of the swamp is covered by some three feet of water, the level varies in other portions. Rarely does it exceed four feet except in small pools or gator holes. The bay is artesian-fed with water pure enough to drink.

While the depths of the bay show virtually no signs of man's intrusion, one cannot escape the sounds of civilization even in the deepest parts. When J. C. Truluck of Olanta, who has probably spent more time in the bay than any other person, and I waded into the marsh one Saturday

1. Just beyond this pool begins a stretch of swamp known as Moccasin Alley because of the large number of poisonous cottonmouth moccasin snakes frequently seen there.

2. A tree frog clings to the bark of a gum tree, while swaying Spanish moss clings to the other side of the tree.

2

morning in April, the sounds of farm tractors plowing fields for corn and cotton crops filled the air. For the swamp is surrounded by cultivated farmland.

The bay is oval-shaped, and from the air looks like an impression made by a giant egg. Immediately adjacent to it is another impression in the earth's crust virtually the same shape and size. It is known as Dial's Bay; but this bay was drained, timbered, and converted to rich agricultural land. It was partly the loss of Dial's Bay that stirred up conservationists to preserve Woods Bay in its natural state in the early 1970s.

Spearheading that effort was J. C. Truluck, for whom the bay had been a boyhood haunt. You could see him with either a shotgun or a fishing pole about every day heading down the dusty lane from his Olanta home to what he called his "secret swamp."

He would arrive early and stay late, spending the day as only a youth alone with nature can, watching bright wood ducks erupting from the surface of the crystal water in a frenzied flight for freedom; a deadly moccasin, tan and menacing, slithering betwen tangled swamp oaks.

Truluck never dreamed it would change. But when he had become an adult and gone away to work as a dental technician in Florence, his favorite place became threatened. The private owners of the swamp were approached with offers from a timber company. They wanted the giant cypress and tupelo and were willing to pay handsome prices. With Dial's Bay already gone, it seemed only a matter of time before Woods Bay also would be farmland. For once the timber was cut, it would be no difficult matter to drain the water and till the land.

That was in early 1971. Truluck began a one-man campaign to save the bay. He made trips to the capitol in Columbia, contacting every agency he knew in an effort to save the swamp. One dead-end followed another. No one seemed very much interested. No one knew the swamp. Years before, Truluck had traded his shotgun for a camera and had thousands of color photographs of the swamp. He began making public speaking engagements at women's clubs, sororities, and civic clubs.

Soon Truluck had gathered the public support he needed. Letters were written, telegrams sent, phone calls made. Everyone from the governor of the state to members of the legislature and agencies which were involved in conservation were contacted. The tide was turning.

"Not that there weren't plenty of pitfalls along the way," recalled Truluck. "But I was confident from the beginning that somehow we could find a way to save the swamp. I just couldn't believe any place as unique as that could be exploited in the interest of a few thousand dollars."

Most of the seven landowners of the swamp wanted to see the swamp preserved and were sympathetic to Truluck's campaign. They were not wealthy enough to make a gift of their land to the state or to a conservation agency, but they would cooperate in every other way they could to give the campaign time to work. Despite huge sums of money offered by the timber company, they refused to sell.

"We just about lost the swamp," Truluck said. "The

timber companies were so confident they would obtain the trees they had already marked many of them. But then word finally came from Columbia that the legislature had earmarked $200,000 to purchase the bay." That wasn't enough, but it certainly was a move in the right direction. But the Federal Bureau of Outdoor Recreation provided another $149,000, bringing the total sum to more than the amount needed to insure the preservation of Woods Bay.

When special ceremonies were held at the site on July 18, 1973, there wasn't a man there prouder than J. C. Truluck. His efforts merited him the Forest Conservationist of the Year Award, presented by the National Wildlife Federation. And he was named first superintendent of the first South Carolina State Nature Park.

As we waded into the marshy end of the bay, it was refreshing to feel the cool water press against my skin. Truluck wore waders, but I prefer to wade in only old clothes and tennis shoes. I could feel the roots entangled on the spongy peat floor, could sense the touch of underwater limbs from titi bushes and the sharp blades of marsh grass brushing against me. A small alligator swam ahead of us, but we saw not a single snake.

"I've never seen a snake in the marsh portion of the bay," said Truluck. "I don't know why. Perhaps it's just not the right type of environment for them . . . perhaps there's not enough food here. But there are plenty of them in the wooded parts."

We waded on, single file, listening to the swish of the water, sometimes stumbling, but always righting ourselves before falling into the water. Occasionally we came to places bridged by masses of roots and algae forming what appeared to be land. As the waves from our trek passed under them, the weeds and bushes shuddered. It reminded me of the Okefenokee Swamp of Georgia—land of the trembling earth.

After we had trudged a mile or more through waist-deep water in the marsh, we returned to our departure point. We drove back out to the lane and up the hard-surface road past the mill pond which had been built on the edge of the swamp around the turn of the century. For many years a mill grinding grits and flour operated there, using the water from the bay to supply the power. Around 1930, however, the mill shut down and never reopened.

The mill pond, as well as the bay, is home to sizable populations of largemouth bass and bream, and there may be a few catfish. Cooters—aquatic turtles—are found in abundance here. Raccoon, opossum, muskrat, bobcat, black bear, banded water snakes, otter, mink, osprey, and southern bald eagle live in the bay. At one time, it's said, wild turkey, cougar, and the ivory-billed woodpecker lived here. Some signs are occasionally found which cause some birdwatchers to believe the ivory-bill still lurks somewhere within the depths of the swamp—signs such as long strips of bark torn from trees.

Shortly after sloughing into the dense stands of cypress and gum trees on the other side of the bay from the marshy area, we came to a watery bath bordered closely on each side by understory. "This," Truluck said, "is Moccasin Alley."

It was near Moccasin Alley that day that I spotted what I

3. The great blue heron is a year-round resident of the bay.

4. Several species of fern are found in Woods Bay, including the royal and the cinnamon (shown here).

3

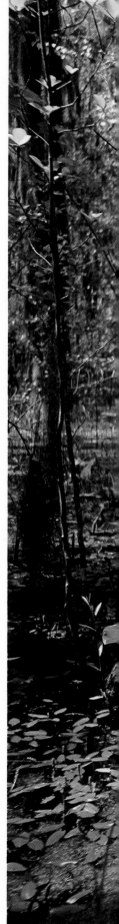

4

5

6

5. *Aerial photograph showing Woods Bay (left) and Dial's Bay, now drained and converted to agriculture.*

6. *In the marsh section of Woods Bay grow rushes, red bay, water lilies, and staggerbush* (shown here), *so named because it sways in the water.*

7. *The marsh portion of Woods Bay is gradually changing into a swamp; already there are islands of woody shrubs and small cypress trees.*

believe to be a world-record cottonmouth snake. At first, it appeared to be the bottomside of a huge turtle turned edgeways in the water. The markings were similar, but when I got closer I noticed the large scales, and then, at least two feet away, I saw the triangular-shaped head, the slit eyes watching my every move. The girth of the snake appeared to be as thick as the calf of my leg, and even as I watched it lying there, I could feel the hair rising on the back of my neck.

Truluck had warned me about the snakes before going into this section of the bay. ''The water will be up to your waist much of the time,'' he had said, ''and if a man were nailed in the chest by one of these big moccasins back there on a hot day like this, there'd be no chance of getting out alive.'' We saw no more snakes that day, but both Truluck and I knew they were there, perhaps within close range.

The Parks Department hopes to establish limited canoe trails through portions of the bay for public use; thus far, there isn't enough space between trees and understory for one to pass. I look forward to that day, as I'm sure many swamp lovers do; for as beautiful and spellbinding as Woods Bay is, those moccasins are just too close for comfort.

CHAPTER
9
The
Great Cypress
Swamp of Delaware

We console ourselves with the comfortable fallacy
that a single museum piece will do,
ignoring the clear dictum of history that a
species must be saved
in many places if it is to be saved at all.

—Aldo Leopold

Cold water squished around my feet and oozed into my shoes as I walked softly across the thick green carpet of soggy sphagnum moss. The sting of autumn filled the air; the trees responded to each breath of the wind, peppering down a shower of multi-colored leaves. In sporadic openings where the canopy of water maple, sweet gum, and sycamore allowed the sun to sift through to the Delaware forest floor, young seedlings of white cedar and bald cypress grew profusely from the quagmire. They represented a new era, for bald cypress had all but disappeared from the Great Cypress Swamp of Delaware years ago. Once these trees had been so plentiful that the swamp took its name from them.

The swamp was dense in most places, allowing an occasional road or trail to pass through its rich understory cluttered with vines, bushes, and briars. A few small streams drained its gushy bottomlands, ultimately converging on the headwaters of the Pocomoke River which wends its way across the Maryland border on the Delmarva Peninsula and saunters toward Chesapeake Bay. Rain runoff and natural springs accounted for much of the swamp's lifeblood, and it, in turn, accounted somewhat for the Pocomoke, one of the East's most scenic rivers, known for its deep, dark waters.

The swamp had all but disappeared a few years ago, however. It is the chief example of a swamp given a new birthright by man. In most cases, it is man who destroys the swamp, conquers it, and turns it to his own use. The Great Cypress, however, was reclaimed by man—not for economical reasons, but for esthetic ones. My companion pointed to the young cypress proudly, for he'd played an important role in reestablishing their growth here.

"Just two years of growth," he said, looking the part of a Delaware wetlands farmer who had just reaped another successful harvest. Freddie Hudson had spent most of his life tilling the rich, dark soil of the Delmarva Peninsula, but in recent years had retired to an even more active role as field representative of one of the most energetic conservation organizations in North America—Delaware Wild Lands, Inc.

Heading up that organization was Ted Harvey, founder and president. At about the time all hope seemed lost for the Great Cypress Swamp, Harvey, who had grown up in Delaware, returned from Florida. As a boy, he had gained a great respect for trees, history, natural beauty, and, above all, the land he called home. Shocked and dismayed by what he saw, he knew something had to be done.

The opportunity presented itself in 1961 when some 1,200 acres of the Great Cypress were put up for sale. Harvey didn't have the purchase price of $80,000, but he started looking for someone who did. Among those he approached with his idea for preserving the Great Cypress for the public was the Wilmington Garden Club. They showed interest, and within weeks Harvey had formed the private, nonprofit Delaware Wild Lands, Inc.

At first, support was slow in coming, but the word gradually circulated and people began to realize the plight of the swamp. For the first few years, all of the money used by the group to acquire and manage their lands came through private donations mainly from wealthy Delawar-

1. *Asters dot the landscape of the Great Cypress in early summer.*

2. *Several types of mosses are common in the Great Cypress, including this rose moss, often found growing around decayed wood.*

3. *Jack-in-the-pulpit, sometimes called Indian turnip, is but one of several varieties of wildflowers found in the Great Cypress.*

4. *In May and June, the aroma of blooming wild roses is added to the many other scents of the swamp.*

1

eans with strong family or business relationships to some of Delaware's leading industrial firms.

Donations, however, ranged from pennies upward and came from individuals in all walks of life. Ted Harvey recalls fondly a crumpled dollar bill that arrived in the mail one day from an old lady who wrote she didn't have much money, but wanted to do a little something to save the Delaware she remembered as a girl.

The Great Cypress is different from other swamps in many ways. Here, as in very few places this far north, you can see and experience a miniature wilderness in which the earth's evolution is suddenly and dramatically alive. Giant bald cypress trees—last of their species to be found at this latitude—tower above the dark, tannin-colored swamp waters. It is a place where a child of any age can imagine the Mesozoic era of our planet's geological history, complete with flying reptiles and dinosaurs. Some eighty million years ago, this swamp, along with sister swamps, actually covered much of the Delmarva Peninsula.

A lot of oldtimers on the Delmarva can remember when land now tended in corn and soybeans was once swampland. The general attitude of most people was that the swamp was good for nothing. Progress had to do away with it, wipe the woodlands clean and drain the water away. Then it could become productive; and that's exactly what happened to much of the 50,000 acres that made up the Great Cypress Swamp of the nineteenth century.

"You know, I once believed the same thing," Freddie Hudson confessed. "After all, it's natural a landowner and farmer would think in those terms. It made more sense to raise corn than bushes. But then I always saw a certain beauty in the swamp, too . . . the dense curtain of woods that marked the boundaries between swampland and farmland."

The gradual conversion of swamplands to agriculture, with its threat to the ecology of the region, continued steadily until the inception of Harvey's organization in 1961. Since that formation, Delaware Wild Lands, Inc., has purchased thousands of acres in different parts of the state including a contiguous plot of 10,000 acres in the center of the Great Cypress Swamp, an area that extends along both banks of the headwaters of the Pocomoke River (from the Algonquin Indian term meaning "black water") and across the state boundary with some 500 acres in Worcester County, Maryland.

Not all the damage to the swamp was done by man, however. The forces of nature played a devastating role, too. In 1930, the swamp, critically dry from periodic drought, caught fire and burned for eight months, smoking up a good section of the East Coast. Residents of towns as far away as Wilmington could smell the swamp burning, and those living closer were forced to keep their windows closed to avoid getting their homes filled with cypress smoke.

Local citizens didn't get much excited about it, though, for the swamp had been on fire many times before and had always burned itself out. This time proved to be different. As days passed, the smoke continued to billow from the morass as the fires spread, people began to fear strong winds might carry the flames to other areas of the Del-

2

4

3

5. *(Overleaf) At Trap Pond State Park are some of the finest examples of what the Great Cypress Swamp of Delaware's Delmarva Peninsula once was.*

6. From the black waters of Trussum Pond, a small turtle seeks a place in the spring sunshine.

7. Northern winds in autumn sweep across the swamp, carrying seeds from pods of milkweed and a thousand other plants to reseed them in another place for the spring thaw.

8. Occasionally the swamp terrain is punctuated with small pools covered with lily pads which bloom in the late spring.

6

7

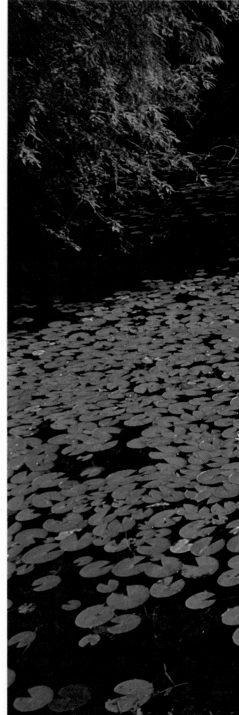

8

marva. Volunteers from all over the peninsula gathered to fight the great fire. Finally, it was reported to be out, only to suddenly flare up again a mile away in the middle of a cornfield. The swamp fire was burning underground through the rich layer of peat moss that had been forming for centuries from decaying vegetable matter.

Great fallen cypress logs, some of them exceeding four feet in diameter at the base, had become buried in the quagmire through the ages. Trees less resistant to water would have decayed, but the cypress remained almost as well preserved as the day, centuries ago, they had fallen. Once the underground fires caught them, they burned for days, smoldering for lack of oxygen, but keeping the coals stored until an ultimate break in the earth's crust allowed the fire to spring to life again.

Long before the great fire of 1930, generations of shingle-makers, aided by yokes of oxen, had mined the fallen cypress and made shingles thirty inches wide or more. Old buildings still stand in Sussex and Kent counties today sheathed with these long-lived, hand-riven shingles. Freddie showed me one standing near the swamp, the shingles bleached ghostlike by the elements, but still in near perfect condition. By 1930, however, the shingle makers had begun importing redwood from the West Coast, and most people forgot about the buried bald cypress.

For eight months, the fires burned before finally being brought under control. By this time, most of the standing timber of the Great Cypress Swamp had been consumed, as well as virtually all of the buried logs. Much of the bald cypress, which reaches its northern terminus at this spot, and the southern white cedar were all but gone. Other endangered species of plants include such exotic flowers as the white-fringed orchid and the fragrant swamp magnolia.

Before the great fire, the swamp was alive with wildlife. Heavy populations of the eastern copperhead snake, mink, otter, muskrat, fox, opossum, raccoon, swamp rabbit, squirrel, chipmunk, and turtle ranged here. With the additional lands preserved by Delaware Wild Lands, in recent years, these populations are beginning to return. Bald eagle, wood duck, American egret, yellow-crowned night heron, and pileated woodpecker are using the area again. Some of them nest here. Other wildlife making a comeback include white-tailed deer, swamp rabbit, and several species of turtle.

The fire was not the last of the swamp's difficulties, however. It was to be further plagued by efforts to drain it. The Great Depression of the 1930s was beginning to be drastically felt about the time the fire was extinguished. The federal government instigated projects using the unemployed to drain the Great Cypress Swamp. In 1936, a twenty-foot-wide canal, fed by ditches, was completed to connect the headwaters of the Pocomoke River with the Indian River. The result was a dry swamp.

The people of the area liked that result. There were fewer mosquitoes and flying insects. They could now hike through the swamp and hunt its wildlife. But this, in fact, became a chain reaction. For with fewer insects, there also were fewer birds. Little did people realize that this region

was unique; this was the last of the large cypress swamps that many millennia ago covered much of the Delmarva Peninsula. Little did they realize, too, that the swamp was a great reservoir of fresh water which acted as a sponge to soak up and hold the rainfall and gradually feed the underground streams of much of Delmarva during the dry seasons.

As a consequence of the inroads made by progress, the Great Cypress Swamp is no longer intact. It may never be. Instead it lies in reclaimed tracts. The best examples lie along a county road just east of Gumboro and at Trussum Pond and Trap Pond State Park near Laurel. Other areas include Ellis Pond on the James Branch, and still other tracts are being added as money and Pepper Pond property become available, the fields replanted in cypress and white pine instead of corn and soybeans.

According to historians, the first explorer from Europe to see the Great Cypress was Giovanni da Verrazano, who called the area "Arcadia" because of the beautiful trees. In a letter to Francis I dated July 8, 1524, he detailed his discoveries and noted the Indian women wore "covering made of certain plants, which hung down from the branches of trees." This, naturalists believe, was clothing made from Spanish moss, which isn't found in the swamp today but may have been there during the sixteenth century.

Verrazano continued his report by describing many of the giant grapevines growing in the swamp: "These vines would doubtless produce excellent wine if they were properly cultivated and attended to, as we have often seen grapes that they produce very sweet and pleasant, and not unlike our own." Verrazano doubtless was describing the muscadine which also reaches its northern boundary in Sussex County, but which grows profusely in the Great Dismal Swamp of Virginia and North Carolina to this day. During colonial times, natives made a wine called "scuppernong" from this grape.

Few people ventured into the Great Cypress Swamp during those early days. Soon after English botanist Thomas Nuttall arrived in the United States in 1808, he visited the swamp and later described it as "one of the most frightening labyrinths you can imagine." But he also collected its flora—thirty-two specimens that he presented to the Academy of Natural Sciences in Philadelphia.

In 1884, this fearful aspect of the Great Cypress became part of American literature in a novel, *The Entailed Hat*, by George Alfred Townsend. It captured some of the legends of the swamp; others came as a result of it.

Over the decades, men have immortalized the swamp with tales of giant turtles and priceless otter skins taken there. As late as the 1930s, years after the mining of bald cypress to be made into shingles was discontinued, a legend celebrated the "Old Man of the Swamp," the best shingle-maker who ever swung a holly mallet. On cloudy days, you could sometimes hear the Old Man, deep in the swamp, regularly riving out his shingles, hour after hour, just as he had years before.

Although fires, drainage, and man had taken most of what the Great Cypress had to offer by 1940, there remained another valuable timber—white oak. Timbermen

swept through the forests again and again, harvesting and reharvesting until it, too, was all but gone. When the historic American frigate *Constitution* was being rebuilt in 1929, some 500 choice white oaks were taken from the Great Cypress and shipped to Boston for the reconstruction.

The Great Cypress Swamp is tired. We trekked through hammocks of hardwood on ground just above the damp, water-soaked forest floor and sat listening on the banks of little streams feeding the canals carrying water away from the swamp. Freddie Hudson told me Delaware Wild Lands hopes to dam those ditches and canals someday, thereby controlling the amount of water released from the swamp. "It is, as anyone can plainly see," he said, "like a bleeding artery; until the flow is stopped, or at least controlled, the swamp will never be the same again. Without water, we cannot even grow transplanted cypress and white cedar."

It appeared that nature had given the Great Cypress a healing hand, for the dense curtain that stood drawn at the edge of crop fields was like an impenetrable jungle bearing few scars noticeable to a newcomer. The blackened char of the fires had long ago been rinsed away by season after season of heavy rains. And the jungle had begun to recapture the lands being converted back from farmland to swamp.

The silence of the thicket was shattered by the yammer of a pileated woodpecker somewhere in the forest. And the words of Ted Harvey, who possesses a great affection for this land rang in my mind: "Our generation," he said, "may well be the last which can exercise free choice of what can be saved of our dwindling natural areas. Let us accept this as a challenge to our good taste, to our responsibility to the future and to our wisdom. Above all, let us not be short-sighted."

9. *This swamp marks the northern limit of the bald cypress.*

CHAPTER
10
The Big Thicket

When we consider the value of a piece
of land like the Big Thicket, we must never
forget to consider this: What is the value
of a sunset? What is the value of the right to
roam or to simply have a place in nature
where man can refresh his spirit? These are
things that we cannot buy on the
New York Stock Exchange.

—Walter J. Hickel

It was early morning on a spring day in 1973 when I first began my search for the Big Thicket. Driving west and north out of Beaumont, Texas, I purposely took the back roads. According to some of the literature I had studied, the Big Thicket actually began just outside the city limits and extended for miles through the low bayou country. But after four hours and many miles of relentless pursuit, I became frustrated; for the Big Thicket was not to be found, and yet, it was all around me. Or at least it once had been. Most of the Big Thicket had all but disappeared by the latter half of the twentieth century. To find it, one must look most carefully.

In one of the earliest written accounts of the Big Thicket, Gideon Lincecum, a doctor who came to Texas in the 1830s from Mississippi, recorded in his journal on February 9, 1835:

"This day passed through the thickest woods I ever saw. It perhaps surpasses any country in the world for brush. There are eight or ten kinds of green undergrowth, privy, holly, three or four sorts of bay, wild peach trees, bayberry, etc., and so thick you could not see a man 20 yards for miles. The soil is pretty good and the water the very best . . ."

When the Alabama-Coushatta Indians, whose reservation is now a part of the Big Thicket, first came to this area around 1800, the Thicket embraced some three million acres in a dozen or more counties. It was easy to find even 100 years later, for it was a formidable, dense curtain of jungle that seemingly stretched forever. Today the area is generally conceded to lie principally in five east Texas counties—Hardin, Polk, Liberty, Tyler, and Jasper. At least, that's where the U.S. Park Service says it is. In a 1965 study, they used for boundaries the Neches River on the east, the Trinity River on the west, U.S. 90 on the south, and U.S. 190 on the north. Within this area lie the most intriguing parts of what remains of the Texas Big Thicket. But also within this area are a lot of grazing land and farmland that bear no resemblance to what was once the Big Thicket.

Despite man's long, ruthless campaign to convert this wild place to commerce, however, remnants of the Big Thicket do indeed still exist, even if they are difficult for the newcomer to find. And in the autumn of 1974 when this remarkable Big Thicket wilderness had already reached the eleventh hour of its existence, the U.S. Congress gave it a new lease on life by creating the Big Thicket National Preserve. By so doing, it bought some time for conservationists and environmental organizations which, for years, had campaigned for its preservation. As one member of the Big Thicket Association pointed out: "The battle has not yet been won, but victory looms upon the horizon."

By spring of 1975 boundaries had been determined around 84,550 acres in twelve units by the National Park Service, most of the huge lumber companies owning land in those areas had declared a cutting moratorium, and the establishment of the Big Thicket National Preserve—a new designation—was well underway. Congress declared the Park Service must establish the preserve in six years.

1

1. Numerous swamp grasses and sedges grow in the Big Thicket; species normally found only in the East merge here with species from the West, making it a biological crossroads.

2

3

5

4

2. Along the roadsides in the Big Thicket in April are blooms of firewheel, sometimes called Indian blanket.

3. An immature longleaf pine, common in much of the southeastern and southern U.S. The longleaf pine is dependent upon frequent fire in order to reseed itself.

4. Palmetto is one of the principle understory plants found in the Big Thicket.

5. Bladderwort is another of the interesting plants found in the Big Thicket. Its minute traps catch small invertebrates such as the Daphnia. Bladderworts have also been known to contain water meal, a small aquatic plant, which makes the bladderwort herbivorous as well.

6. (Overleaf) Although a great many pines grow in the Big Thicket, there are also dense stands of cypress trees.

The Big Thicket once occupied an area roughly resembling a triangle across the Sabine River from Louisiana. It extended across the basins of three rivers—the Trinity, the Neches, and the Sabine. But it has been diminishing for many years as the demand for timber and oil, grazing and real estate grows. By the late 1930s, two-thirds of the Big Thicket had actually disappeared. And by the 1970s it encompassed no more than 300,000 acres, but it still contains many of the elements of green solitude and untamed beauty, the remote and mysterious regions, that characterized its original state.

In the early days, the Big Thicket held vast deposits of oil, extensive supplies of marketable timber, and many fur-bearing animals. Game was plentiful. At one time on Pigeon Roost Prairie, the passenger pigeons were so thick during migration that people in nearby Kountze claimed that at night they could hear the tree branches cracking under the weight of the birds. The passenger pigeon is now extinct, of course, the last known specimen expiring in the Cincinnati Zoo in 1914. The ivory-billed woodpecker might still live here in large numbers had the timber not been cut and major portions of the swamp drained for agriculture and real estate development. The forest tracts that remain are mostly orderly pine plantations planted and cultivated by the wood pulp companies. The wildness in such places is gone, it would seem, forever. Even some of the oil fields have been pumped dry.

The Thicket over the years was logged and logged again. Early efforts were closely related to the development of mainline railroads through the area. Pine forests were the first to be cut. Hundreds of miles of tramlines were extended from branch lines into the virgin forest. Only quality pines—most of them loblolly for lumber and by-products—were taken then. Hardwoods would come later. The Thicket was left a chaos of dead treetops; and because of the matted dead brush, fires soon became a hazard also, destroying much of what was left. By 1935, virtually all of the original Big Thicket pine forest had been cut. Today, only a few virgin loblolly pine trees may be seen in the more remote areas.

At the town of Evadale is evidence of what the Thicket produces today. If you can stomach the stench of a vast paper mill, you'll see here an operation of the Eastex Company, a subsidiary of Time Inc., its vast yards filled with towering piles of hardwood logs, many of them cut from the Big Thicket. To some of the local people, the mill smells of money; to others who would remember or imagine the Thicket in its natural state, it's the smell of destruction.

Despite this, the Big Thicket is an area of contrast and surprise, an ecotone—a biological crossroad where a wide variety of plant communities meet and intermingle, plants found in the tropics, some characteristic of the desert—and some from the Appalachians. Geraldine Watson, a naturalist who has been most ardent in efforts to save the Big Thicket, counts seven distinct plant associations here—savannahs, upland communities, beech-magnolia communities, floodplain forests, baygalls, palmetto—bald-cypress–hardwood communities, bogs—with a few thousand species. For instance, there are twenty-six ferns;

five of North America's six genera of carnivorous plants, including sundew and pitcher plants; and forty species of orchids. There are cactus and yucca, sphagnum moss, huge cypress and sweet gum, and great oaks with the resurrection fern growing along their branches.

Yes, the Big Thicket might be called one of America's most unusual swamps—and yet it is more than a swamp. It contains, according to a report by the National Park Service, elements common to the Okefenokee Swamp, the Florida Everglades, the Piedmont forests, the Appalachians, and the open woodlands of the coastal plains.

The late Lance Rosier, who spent all his life in his beloved Big Thicket and for whom the 25,024-acre Lance Rosier Unit of the National Preserve was named, used to call it a "hodgepodge." The Thicket, he would say in his sojourns through the wet woodlands, is a little bit of everything. Rosier, fondly known in east Texas as Mr. Big Thicket, spent a great part of his life campaigning for the preservation of the Big Thicket; unfortunately he never lived to see it become a reality.

Perhaps the greatest hope for preservation for the Big Thicket, however, lies in the fact that it is among the last potential domains of the ivory-billed woodpecker, considered extinct by many authorities since the 1920s, and of the endangered Texas red wolf. Both have been sighted here in recent years. Ornithologist John Dennis of the Nature Conservancy has no doubts at all he spotted an ivory-bill in 1966, and Mrs. Dollie Hoffman of Saratoga, Texas, a lifelong resident and friend of Rosier, claims to have seen one in the early 1970s. Sometimes the preservation of such a wild place hinges upon the effort to save an endangered species of wildlife.

For many years a battle raged over how much of the Big Thicket should be preserved in its natural state—or whether it should be preserved at all. Lined up on one side was a group of active conservationists and on the other, primarily, a handful of timber companies which owned most of the land—the Kirby Lumber Co., a subsidiary of the Atcheson, Topeka, and Santa Fe Railroad; and Temple Industries and Eastex, both subsidiaries of Time Inc., the New York–based magazine publishers, which controlled more than 1.5 million acres of land in the Big Thicket and the adjoining area. Other smaller companies were involved, too, but their combined holdings did not equal those of the three larger companies.

Part of the concern of the conservationists, acting primarily through the Big Thicket Association with headquarters at Saratoga, was over an area of tree giants, many of them national or state champions. For in the Big Thicket grow the world's largest red bay, sweetleaf, black hickory, American holly, planer-tree, sparkleberry, eastern red cedar, and two-wing silverbell. It is quite natural that the Big Thicket should produce such outstanding and varied examples of plant life, for it encompasses a great variety of soils.

A range of low hills runs along its northern border with an underlying base of Miocene rock. From there it slopes down to form a great basin filled to a depth of thousands of feet with fertile black soil mixed with fine sandy loams deposited during the Pleistocene period. The water table

7. *The insectivorous pitcher plant grows in wet, sandy or peaty soils, usually in full sun. This particular species is Sarracenia alata.*

8 and 9. *Details of pitcher plant flower.*

10. *The hooded pipelike pitchers wait for insects attracted by their sweet odor, to crawl into the stem.*

11. *Once the insect has reached the sticky substance, the plant secretes at the bottom of its stem, it's too late to turn back. The feet are glued and the plant begins to devour the insect, as shown here at the bottom of a pitcher.*

7

remains high and rainfall is heavy with about sixty inches a year. The elevation, ranging between sea level and 400 feet above sea level, permits only sluggish drainage. With Gulf winds to maintain a year-round moderate climate, the Big Thicket has all the necessary ingredients for tremendous growth and a botanical paradise.

The Thicket's vegetation ranges from a dense dark curtain of junglelike forest beyond which one has difficulty even seeing, much less walking, to palmetto plains that grow high enough to hide a man on horseback. Occasionally one comes to a swampy baygall (a wetlands area with a heavy growth of white bay trees and gallberry holly shrubs) infested with cottonmouth moccasins. Travel through the baygalls is almost impossible, for they are intertwined with laurel-leaf smilax, poison ivy, and muscadine grapevines.

One of the most fascinating and persistent legends of the Big Thicket is the Ghost Road near the village of Votaw in Hardin County. People have come many miles to see it, some of them armed and ready to shoot at anything they suspect to be a ghost. Legend claims that a railway brakeman was beheaded by the wheels of a passing train, and that his ghost stalks the woods nearly every night with a lantern, looking for its head. Some people claim their automobiles have been chased by great balls of fire during the night on this road. Others claim the light is merely gas with a fluorescent quality emitted from the swamp.

During the Civil War, the Thicket proved a refuge for a group of men who had no desire to fight in slavery's cause. Hiding in the forest, they were later discovered and surrounded in a five-acre area and ordered to surrender. Confederate Captain John Kaiser ordered the area burned when they refused, to this day this area is known as Kaiser's Burnout. The fate of the fugitives remains uncertain; no trace of them was ever found.

Over the years the Big Thicket has seen relatively few visitors. Diaries dating from the early Spanish missions tell how all the trails skirted around this place. Later, pioneers traveling west through the region were discouraged by the impenetrable jungle. Over a span of three centuries the Big Thicket provided a hideout, first for Indians, later for outlaws, runaway slaves, and army deserters. According to one story, Sam Houston, during the Texas Revolution, planned to disappear with his army into this wild sanctuary if he lost the Battle of San Jacinto. Those who took refuge here lived off the land—wild game and wild honey—there's even a town named Honey Island where fugitives brought honey to be traded on the black market for goods and wares they needed in the swamp.

The Thicket has always been a sanctuary for various types of wildlife as well. Besides the ivory-bill and the red wolf, there also are such rarities as Swainson's warbler, the red-cockaded woodpecker, pileated woodpeckers, and virtually the only black bear found in all of eastern Texas. There are bobcat and possibly panther. As late as the 1930s, jaguar and the Mexican ocelot were counted as regular inhabitants of the swamp.

Before one treks off through the Thicket, he should be well versed in the area as well as being a good woodsman. For the peaceful green solitude that lies just beyond the

8

9

10

11

jungle curtain can be deceiving and treacherous. Many a person has ventured into the Thicket for no more than what he considered a few feet, never to return again. Guides are available either through the Big Thicket Association or through the Alabama-Coushatta Indian Reservation along the Big Thicket's northern edge.

Besides such poisonous snakes as the cottonmouth moccasin and eastern copperhead, there also are timber, canebrake, and pygmy rattlers, and coral snakes. Wild hogs are another potential danger.

''In many ways the Big Thicket is like the spiderweb to an insect,'' explains Dollie Hoffman. It will betray you . . .''

Along the Neches River, one finds still a different Big Thicket amid dense stands of trees draped with clambering vines of muscadine grapes, coils of pepper vines, and wild wisteria. And it's along the Neches and Trinity that you'll likely find the greatest number of large birds such as the egret, Louisiana heron, green heron, and great blues. At times the Neches is shallow, almost impossible for a canoe or johnboat to navigate. At other times, holes run forty feet deep.

The Big Thicket is a place of timeless and unpredictable beauty—what's left of it. Justice William O. Douglas wrote in his *Farewell to Texas* in 1967 that there is hope that with increasing education ''a new generation will realize the awful destruction which the lumber companies, the oil companies, the real estate developers, the road builders and the poachers have wreaked on one of the loveliest areas with which God blessed this nation.''

12. The ivory-billed woodpecker. Thought by many to be extinct, the ivory-bill has been spotted several times in recent years in the Big Thicket.

13. More than a hundred species of wildflowers are found in the Big Thicket, among them ground phlox and evening primrose (lower right).

14. The Big Thicket is made up of sloughs, soggy wetlands, and mirrorlike pools, amid dense forests.

12

13

CHAPTER
11
Hawaii's Alakai

The best way to remember a place is to go back,
and to find it no less than it was.
There are still a few places . . . you can go back to
and be pleased how well you remember them and
how wildness cared for them while
you were gone.

—David R. Brower

In the shadow of Mount Waialeale along a crested valley of the paradise island of Kauai lies the Alakai Swamp, which the native Hawaiians once called the "swamp in the clouds." It is virtually that, for often the Alakai is shrouded with mists and fog. Most of the islands of Hawaii were created by volcanic action, and Alakai has the distinction of being the only swamp located in the crater of a volcano.

On the topographic maps compiled by the U.S. Geological Survey, the Alakai is listed as a swamp, but authorities say that, with the exception of half a dozen or so bog areas, it does not fit the generally accepted description of a swamp. Located on a kind of plateau surrounded on three sides by precipitous cliffs, Alakai is far too well drained to fit the standard description of a swamp. Yet it probably possesses far more swamplike qualities than any other, so for our purposes we will consider it as the Hawaiians have for ages—swamp.

The word "alakai" in Hawaiian means "one-file track," a term obviously referring to the dense growth in the swamp which permitted only single-file entry. Within a mile of its southeastern boundary is Mount Waialeale, which experiences the heaviest rains on earth—a documented annual accumulation of somewhere in the vicinity of 460 to 470 inches, or nearly forty feet. The swamp itself gets something less than that, probably around 200 to 225 inches.

The Alakai, approximately nine miles long and three miles wide, is about 4,000 feet above sea level, well above the range of the troublesome mosquito. Until recent years, little was known about the swamp except that it was there. Aircraft pilots flew over it and noted the extraordinary green jungle canopy, but no one ever penetrated its dense understory where giant ferns grow twenty feet tall and moss clings a foot thick on the trunks of the trees. The principal tree there is the ohia lehua, which grows no more than fifty feet tall because of the saturated condition of the clay and peat soil. (It normally grows eighty feet or more in height.) In some places, the trees are even more stunted because of the heavier water content in the soil. Peat layers generally range about a foot over most of the Alakai, but at some spots are more than four feet deep.

For centuries the Alakai has been largely inaccessible. The general topography and the densely entangled junglelike growth was enough to discourage all but the most determined hikers. On three sides steep cliffs, called *palis* in Hawaiian, bound the swamp, but there are a few approaches with less steep ridges. Long ago Hawaiian natives climbed these ridges en route to Mount Waialeale for worship ceremonies. A stone heap (*heiau*) still exists today at the summit of the mountain where these religious ceremonies were held overlooking the vastness of the swamp. Today the Alakai is accessible only by helicopter or by foot from the southwestern side where the terrain slopes more gently to the basin of the Waimea River.

The rains are another reason the Alakai remains largely unexplored by man. "It scares people to think of experiencing a thirty-inch rainfall in twenty-four hours," said an official of the U.S. Forest Service Pacific Institute in Honolulu. "And that's what happens in the swamp. It can rain so hard up there, you think you're swimming underwater."

The rain water disappears quickly, however, soaking rapidly into the peat soil or being carried off through a series of deeply gashed streams that lead to the cliffs and downward to other jungles below. The streams through the ages have slashed their way into narrow canyons, some only a few feet wide and as much as 500 feet deep. Fog is a factor, too, and often comes without warning, even when there are no rains. "If the right atmospheric pressures and the right temperatures prevail, you can bet there's going to be a fog in the Alakai," said Tom Telfer of the Hawaii Division of Fish and Game, "even when there's fog nowhere else. When it's not actually raining, the air is full of thick white mist, the sky is toad-belly gray, and there's rarely a glimpse of the sun or the stars."

Consequently, it's easy to become lost in the Alakai, and a good many of those who mustered enough courage to enter have never returned. In other forests one can sometimes get a bearing by finding moss that grows only on the north side of the trees, but in the Alakai a light green moss grows in such profusion all around the tree that one may have difficulty even touching the tree itself or digging into it. An open season on feral pigs brings hunters to the Alakai, however; sometimes one of them discovers the rusted remains of a gun and some scattered bones belonging perhaps to another hunter who had ventured there previously, lost his way, and ultimately his life.

Telfer, who does considerable research and study of wildlife in the Alakai, comes and goes mostly by helicopter. He's never been seriously lost in the swamp, but admits it could happen. On the mainland, he said, the general rule is to find a stream and follow it. Ultimately it's going to lead to a settlement or a road; but that's not true here. If you follow a stream in the Alakai, it likely will only lead you to a high waterfall pouring over the side of a cliff, one you cannot climb down. So here you follow the ridges, not the streams.

John Sincock of the U.S. Fish and Wildlife Service, who for years studied several species of endangered birds found only in the Alakai, tells of another danger in the swamp, from the vicious and unpredictable pig. "Once when I had been in the swamp for about a week, I was down on my stomach in the muck, crawling under a fallen tree, when I came face to face with a pig," he said. "He was so close I could smell his breath. Meanest goddam pig I ever saw, about three hundred pounds of sinew and hide so tough you probably couldn't cut it with a razor. And those big yellow tusks! I'll never forget the sight of them. One of us had to get out of the way, so I started back to oblige him. But do you know, I looked worse and smelled worse than the pig did, so he backed up to get out of my way."

Sincock himself has had some close calls in the swamp, even though he has become, over the years, sensitive to the dangers involved. Once while intently following the call of a bird, he fell thirty feet into a ravine and smashed a leg. He bound the leg with plastic tape he normally carries to mark his trail into the swamp, but he knew immediately he would never walk out. The pain was excruciating.

Dragging himself to an opening, he lay down in the rain, hoping sometime soon the sky would clear and a helicopter might come looking for him. For two days he lay there, soaked and in a near state of shock, before the helicopter was able to find him. Two months later he was able to walk without crutches.

The other major animals found in the swamp are feral goats, ugly creatures almost as large as men with huge splayed feet which enable them to walk on the spongy peat surface. It is not these which attract the most attention to Alakai, however, but instead a half-dozen or so species of nearly extinct birds. Among them are the Drepanididae (honeycreepers), the small Kauai thrush (found only in the Alakai where it lives a largely secretive life), the Elepaio or Hawaiian flycatcher, the Kauai oo, the sicklebills or Hawaiian woodpecker, and the ou thickbill. Several of these species were once found throughout the Hawaiian Islands, but now are only found in the Alakai Swamp and then only rarely.

The Alakai Swamp, one of the last remaining native forest preserves in the Hawaiian Islands, seems to be in a state of transition. Foresters are concerned about a changing ecosystem in the swamp where heavy infiltrations of blackberry vines, firebush, and lantana weeds are moving

1

112

2

Tom Telfer

1. *Young tree ferns or fiddleheads.*

2. *Wild boar, found throughout the Alakai, are among the most dangerous creatures there.*

3. *The Alakai is actually a high rain forest with jungle growth so dense you can hardly pass through it.*

4. *This native honeycreeper, caught in a mist net installed by biologists to enable them to band the bird for studies before releasing it into the wild again, is found nowhere else in the world.*

3

Tom Telfer

4

into certain areas. Wherever a clearing develops, either by fire, uprooted trees, or the ruthless rootings of feral hogs, weeds and vines capture the area with growths so dense nothing else can survive. Robert Nelson, director of the Institute of Pacific Islands Forestry of the U.S. Forest Service in Honolulu believes this could have critical results in the Alakai and perhaps an ultimate devastating effect upon its endangered wildlife.

The State Division of Forestry has begun a program of control against such intrusions and, hopefully, it will become effective enough to maintain some sort of stability in the delicate ecological system of the Alakai. But it will most likely be a continuing battle. That is the principle reason a hunting season is allowed on the feral pigs—a matter of control against undue damage to the forest.

In the summer of 1960, Dr. Frank Richardson, professor of zoology at the University of Washington, and his assistant, John Bowles, made an extensive study of the bird life on Kauai and particularly in the Alakai. At that time, they discovered several species—the puajohi, alkaloa, nukupuu, and ou—thought to be extinct, giving Kauai the distinction of being the only island in the chain with all its native bird populations intact. Dr. Richardson immediately urged that the Alakai be set aside as a special sanctuary and that stringent measures be taken to protect this unique area from the encroachment of exotic plants which might alter their habitat.

It was more than three years later that Jim Ferry, then chairman of the State Department of Land and Natural Resources, organized a committee of scientists and charged it with the task of coming up with a recommendation for the preservation of the Alakai. He gave them just thirty days. They acted, and in January 1964 the Board of Land and Natural Resources established a regulation which gives the Alakai that protection.

Visitors to the Alakai are few, and those who do hike in usually do not stay overnight. They are not encouraged to do so, for increased use may create additional problems. The best time to go is October and November; later in the winter it is bitterly cold in the Alakai and sometimes it snows there.

Because of its remote geographical character, because of its dense growth and heavy rains, the Alakai will likely remain a Garden of Eden largely undisturbed by man for many years to come. It is forbiddingly beautiful on a clear day, but the swamp has only a few of those. Many of those who know the swamp best are convinced that as long as the rare birds of Kauai do indeed continue to exist, they will be found in the Alakai. For them, it is a very special paradise.

5

6

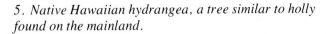

5. Native Hawaiian hydrangea, a tree similar to holly found on the mainland.

6. Typical tree fern understory in an ohia forest.

Partridge pea.

CHAPTER
12
Honey Island Swamp

It is a place that seems often unable to
make up its mind whether it
will be earth or water, and so it compromises.

—Harnett T. Kane
The Bayous of Louisiana

Along the matted root banks of the meandering Pearl River Basin east of New Orleans is one of the least-explored swamps in America—Honey Island. Honey Island Swamp, an area approximately fifty miles long and five miles at its widest point, is the domain of the mosquito, the wild hog, poisonous snakes, and reputedly an unidentified creature they call "The Thing."

Located in both Mississippi and Louisiana, with the greater portion in the latter, Honey Island Swamp and its river basin is a primitive wilderness of tupelo, oak, and bald cypress which provide such a dense canopy that little understory is able to survive. Thus the swamp has the appearance of being open and laced with numerous waterways that turn and twist and lead nowhere in particular. Closer to the Gulf of Mexico the swamp turns into tidal marsh; the trees give way to marsh grasses and canebrake.

During the warm months, the swamp is a dank and dark jungle; in winter the southern end is a haven for migrating waterfowl. There are a few recently opened canoe trails in parts of the swamp, but the trails only begin to explore the swamp or to capture its atmosphere. There are parts of Honey Island where man has never set foot.

In the early 1970s the Louisiana Wildlife and Fisheries Commission purchased 15,594 acres of the swamp in St. Tammany Parish as a wildlife sanctuary. Aside from that, much of the swamp is owned by timber interests and land-holding companies, but most of it is open to the public.

Honey Island is watered by the Pearl, West Pearl, and Middle Pearl Rivers, in addition to numerous sloughs and bayous. None of its lakes are deep, but there is enough water for the largemouth bass, sac-a-lait, perch, bream, and catfish.

It is to these pools that many of the wading birds—ibis, great blue herons, and egrets—come to feed. And in winter, there are thousands of ducks which have migrated down the Mississippi flyway to escape the cold weather. In spring, they leave again for the return trip north. Among those that do not fly north are the wood duck, permanent nesters in Honey Island. Many of the waterfowl congregate in the marsh section of the swamp along the Gulf estuaries.

The northernmost portions of the swamp are the densest. The land is higher and the plant communities are somewhat different, including considerably more understory. Here the swamp is characterized by stands of water-, willow-, cow-, overcup-, and turkey-oak. It's in this section, too, that the unnamed creature of the swamp reputedly roams. Several people have seen the creature during the past few years, and all descriptions are similar. It stands about seven feet tall, weighs an estimated 400 pounds, leaves four-toed tracks in the mud, and is covered all over with short, gray hair. The scalp hair, however, hangs down more than two feet long. It walks semiupright, but has razor sharp claws that could rip flesh to bits.

Plaster of paris casts have been made of the creature's footprints, enough to indicate there are several creatures and not just one. All of the people who have seen it at various times have indicated it appeared unlike anything

1

4

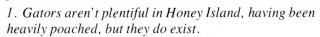

2

3

5   6

1. *Gators aren't plentiful in Honey Island, having been heavily poached, but they do exist.*

2. *A Louisiana heron strikes at a small bream in the shallows of the swamp. Often the water is not clear enough to permit wading birds to see their prey.*

3. *The heron's efforts pay off.*

4. *Pileated woodpeckers are found in virtually all swamps of the United States and particularly those of the South.*

5. *A golden orb spider, sometimes measuring three inches across, waits for a meal to fly into its web.*

6. *Once the meal is entangled in the web, the golden orb quickly weaves a cocoon around its prey.*

7. *Water levels from the fluctuating Pearl River complex can be seen on the trunks of the tupelo gum.*

they had ever seen, as though it were something left over from prehistoric times.

Two men said they had found two large wild hogs with their throats ripped out, presumably by The Thing. Biologists and anthropologists from several Louisiana universities have examined the casts, but made no positive identification; and many people, including scientists, are skeptical of its existence.

The creature is not reported throughout the swamp, but only in the seldom visited northernmost portions. Frank Davis of Louisiana's Wildlife and Fisheries Commission in New Orleans said the mysterious creature, whether fact or fiction, is very real to most of the people who live around the swamp.

"It's understandable," he said, "so many legends should surround such a place, for this is one of the . . . wildest swamps still around today . . . it's very easy to become lost in there . . ."

As late as 1850, Honey Island was a place of refuge for several pirate ships which pillaged the Gulf and the Caribbean. The leader of one such pirate ship was Pierre Rameau, widely known as the King of Honey Island. Born and reared in Scotland, his real name was McCullough, and he maintained a fine home in New Orleans where he was known by that name, but at Honey Island, he was known only as Pierre Rameau.

In 1855 the Copeland gang made their headquarters at Honey Island, too, and terrorized many communities throughout Louisiana, Mississippi, and Alabama, reputedly bringing their stolen wares—mostly gold and jewelry from wealthy plantation owners—to Honey Island where they buried it. In 1857 the leader of the gang—James Copeland—was captured in a shoot-out with law officers at Augusta, Miss. Several members of his gang were killed and the others arrested. Copeland himself was lynched and, as far as can be determined, the gold and jewelry was never recovered. Many people believe it is still buried at Honey Island.

At the turn of the century, timber-cutting operations were conducted in the lower reaches of Honey Island Swamp, the logs floated downstream to mills at Logtown on the Pearl River and Pearlington on the East Pearl. Virtually nothing is left of Logtown today except the ruins, but at one time one of the largest sawmills in the South was located there. While the timber cutting was clearing out select trees in the swamp, farmers decided to try to utilize parts of the swamp for their farming operation. They turned hogs and cattle loose and let them roam free. It is from this livestock that the wild hogs of Honey Island are descended. They live on acorns and roots, and it's difficult to go anyplace in the swamp today without seeing signs of their rooting. On the edge of the swamp is the Mississippi test facility of NASA, where tests are performed on rocket engines used to power space vehicles.

Some lumbering continues to this day on a very limited scale, but most of the big trees were cut years ago. And the farms that were established in the swamp before the turn of the century disappeared with the big flood of 1900 that drowned livestock and washed away buildings and equipment. There are few reminders today of the swamp ever being anything but just that—swamp. The majority of families who lived there have never returned.

7

CHAPTER
13
The Big Cypress and Corkscrew Sanctuary

Deer . . . led us through a dream world
of gray cypresses and silent Spanish moss and soft
knee-deep watery sloughs . . . I stood
and stared and could not believe that I held
orchids in my hands.
—Marjorie Kinnan Rawlings
Cross Creek

The Big Cypress, lying just to the north of the Everglades in southern Florida, is an intricate mosaic of marsh and lowland forest—a wilderness of jungle-shrouded sloughs and bay and cypress heads. Cypress dominates, of course, giving the area its name. Across virtually the entire expanse of what today is considered the Big Cypress Swamp are stands of cypress trees. Those, interspersed with wet prairies and pine ridges, essentially compose the landscape here.

The entire Big Cypress area is underlain with limestone, as is the Florida Everglades. Deposits of peat have built up soil in many places, sometimes atop marl rock, but the limestone outcroppings are evident at many places throughout the swamp. It is the impervious limestone that provides a base for the ecosystem of the Big Cypress. Without it the water would quickly filtrate into the soil and disappear from the surface. But because of this hard limestone pan and because the slope of the terrain in all of south Florida is almost imperceptible to the eye, drainage is very slow. The fact that it lingers makes the Big Cypress an important reservoir not only for its own inhabitants and plant life, but for the western portion of the neighboring Everglades National Park.

Since water plays such an important role in the ecosystems of this entire area, it's important that we dwell in some detail on how it works. There are three generalized patterns of drainage in the Big Cypress. In the northeast, an area mostly included today in the Seminole Indian Reservation, drainage is diverted eastward by a low, nearly imperceptible ridge, extending from the Hendry-Collier county line north of what was once to be a giant jetport. In the west, flow is through a system of canals that diverts water both westward to the Gulf and southward to the bays of the Ten Thousand Islands. Throughout the rest of the Big Cypress, drainage is generally southward and tends to concentrate in Okaloachoochee Slough, the Barron River and Turner River Canals, as well as the Fakahatchee Strand.

This area of Florida has only two seasons—wet and dry. The dry season occurs from late October to May or early June. If enough water is not stored up in the wetland prairies, the holes and ponds and sloughs during the summer wet season, there simply won't be enough to sustain life during the long dry season. Toward the end of the dry season, the wildlife congregates around the remaining waterholes not only for water, but for food, for they prey upon one another. The fewer and smaller the holes, the greater the concentration, and fewer animals, birds, reptiles, and fish will survive until the wet season arrives.

The greatest displays of wildlife drama occur during the final few weeks of the dry season (normally in April and May), when fires set by lightning, by the terrifically hot sun which causes spontaneous combustion in places where debris has collected, or by man help to drive whatever wildlife has not migrated out of the area to the limited water compounds. It is indeed a battle then for survival. Alligators are the kings of the Big Cypress and take their toll from whatever birds or animals come to their watering hole. Sometimes, perhaps driven by hunger, they will prey upon one another. By the time the fires are extinguished by the rains and water dispersal begins a new cycle, there may be only a single huge alligator in each particular waterhole—the lone survivor of all that came that way.

So the ecology of the Big Cypress is water-dominated. During the peak of the wet season (normally in August and September) as much as 90 percent of the undrained area is inundated; during the peak of the dry season, as little as 10 percent. But except in rare cases, or in cases of fire, most plants and animals have adapted over the years to the fluctuating seasonal water levels.

The major plant communities in the Big Cypress are divided generally into pine-palm-palmetto forest, wet prairie and marsh, hammock forest, tidal marsh, mangrove swamp, cypress forest, or fresh-water swamp. In general, the hammock and pine-palm-palmetto forests grow on land only several inches to several feet higher than the surrounding wet prairies and cypress forests. The surfaces of these areas may be inundated only briefly after heavy rain. The treeless wet prairies are inundated for longer periods, drying out early in the dry season. Marshes have deeper water than the wet prairies, but they also may become dry toward the end of the dry season.

The densest growth areas in the Big Cypress are the fresh-water swamps dominated by hardwoods and palms, epiphytic ferns, air plants, and orchids. The fresh-water swamps, inundated most of the year, traditionally support high densities of wildlife ranging from species at the bottom of the food chain all the way up. Here are thousands upon thousands of mosquito fish, killifish, gar, bream, largemouth bass, cottonmouth moccasin, brown water snake, and alligator. Densities of fish as high as 5,000 fish per cubic meter of water have been reported. Rattlesnake (pygmy and the eastern diamondback) may come here to water and to feed, too, as the dry season progresses. As many as 350 wading birds—white ibis, great blue heron, snowy egret, and wood stork—have been observed feeding at one small cypress pond less than 150 feet in diameter. Elbow room is at a premium.

Deer, mink, otter, bobcat, Florida panther, and numerous other animals may gather at the fresh-water swamp, too. So during the later stages of the dry season, it is indeed an oasis or haven for virtually every living thing. The broad expanses of wet prairie have been baked into a veritable desert and support little life.

In the hammocks, or tree islands, one finds species that do not require much water. Panther, cottonmouth moccasin, rattlesnake, swamp rabbit, armadillo, white-tailed deer, and various types of birds such as the great barred owl and red-shouldered hawk may find the hammock a special haven. During the day many of these creatures rest in the hammock, venturing out in the evening or at night to feed in neighboring areas. Some of them even travel to the fresh-water swamps and sloughs for drink or food and return to their lairs by the first break of day.

Animal behavior in the Big Cypress is complex and unusual. By the start of the rainy season, many of the wading birds have migrated out of the area leaving only a few stragglers to spend the many wet, rainy months ahead. Most of the white ibis, for example, have left for parts of

1

2

1. During late winter a great many butterflies, among them the swallowtail, gather in the Big Cypress. The best place to find them is on the moist banks of the remaining waterholes.

2. Water lettuce often covers the pools and waterways in Corkscrew and the Big Cypress. Only a freeze will provide a natural kill, and that seldom occurs in south Florida.

3

4

5

6

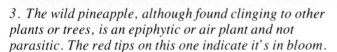

3. *The wild pineapple, although found clinging to other plants or trees, is an epiphytic or air plant and not parasitic. The red tips on this one indicate it's in bloom.*

4. *The Big Cypress in late winter is home to many species of butterfly, including the sulphur (shown here), swallowtail, monarch, and queen.*

5. *The soft lavender blooms of the pickerel weed are found throughout the Corkscrew, Big Cypress, and Everglades.*

6. *The butterfly weed, a species of others found in northern and midwestern states, also grows in Corkscrew Sanctuary.*

7

8

7. *This bird's-nest fern, one of the rarest ferns in America, is believed to grow only in the Big Cypress.*

8. *The Big Cypress is known for orchids. This one is the Ionopsis.*

9. *The strangler fig is one of the most fascinating plants in south Florida's swamps. Often either blown by the wind or carried by a bird, the seeds frequently are deposited in the crotch or branch of another tree. The fig first begins to grow as an air plant. Then it develops roots hanging vinelike toward the ground. Once they reach the ground and penetrate it, the fig tree begins to grow, wrapping its roots around the trunk of the tree which gave it birth, until it cuts off the flow of sap, killing the other tree.*

10. *A hoary air plant clings to the bark of a pine.*

11. *This vine, which twines around itself, is known as the "love vine."*

9

10

11

12. *The Bauer fern.*

13. *The whisk fern, found in both the Big Cypress and Corkscrew, is one of the oldest living plant species. Botanists say it dates back as much as three million years.*

14. *The resurrection fern and clamshell orchid grow side by side in Corkscrew Sanctuary.*

15. *Bird's-nest fern soriferous spores are evident on the bottom side of the leaves and serve as an excellent identification guide.*

16. *This gator hole in the Big Cypress was occupied by a single mother and her babies, but as the dry spell continues, other gators may come to live there, too.*

12

13

14

15

16

17. *Many square miles of the Big Cypress are covered with stunted cypress trees such as these. Botanists say they are stunted because of lack of nutrients in the scanty soil.*

Central America or for nothern climes in Louisiana, the Carolinas, or Virginia. Other smaller and less-mobile forms of wildlife may migrate from one part of the swamp to another.

Those who know the Big Cypress well contend that its plant life is the most interesting of all its complex aspects. In the Fakahatchee Strand (which was being purchased in 1975 by the state of Florida to be preserved), for instance, are thirty-eight species of orchids, seven of which are unique to the Big Cypress area. Many species of fern grow in the area, too, including some found nowhere else on earth.

Park Service Ranger Fred Dayhoff of Ochopee guided me to a cypress head swamp in the Big Cypress one warm day in early February to see what he called the most extraordinary plant in the area. It was the bird's-nest fern, and Fred, who has spent most of his life in the Big Cypress, said he knew of no others anywhere.

"You must promise me," he urged, "you won't divulge the location, though, because every rare plant dealer in Miami would be out here tearing up the countryside looking for them. And they'd find them, too. And dig them up—every last one. Even if they knew these were the very last of the species to be found here, they'd dig them up and carry them away just for a few dollars."

Plant life in the Fakahatchee is unique because it is one of the major forested natural water courses in the Big Cypress. It extends for some twenty miles from a point north of Alligator Alley (a toll highway built during the late 1960s across the Big Cypress from Naples to Fort Lauderdale) to the estuaries near Everglades City and the Gulf of Mexico. The Fakahatchee is actually composed of several channels, numerous lakes, and ponds.

In the past, water entered the Strand from rainfall on nearby drainage area and from the Okaloachoochee Slough which carried water southward from points farther north. But today most of the flow from the Slough has been diverted by canals, and the Fakahatchee is largely dependent upon local rainfall. Consequently, the flora and fauna of the Fakahatchee are changing.

In the late 1940s and early 1950s, the Fakahatchee was heavily lumbered and most of the large cypress tress removed. Trams or elevated lanes of earth were constructed in the swamp to support a narrow-gauge railroad used to remove the giant cypress logs. After logging was completed, the rails were removed, but the trams remained and are now densely forested by hammock vegetation.

Despite the ravages of logging, the Fakahatchee is still a botanical rarity with large oaks, maples, cabbage or Sabal palms, and a variety of tropical trees forming a dense canopy. Royal palms tower above the canopy like natural monuments. A great variety of epiphytes, ferns, vines, and shrubs form a dense understory. Pop ash, pond apple, and cypress dominate the deep-water areas. The strand has long been known as one of the richest anywhere outside the tropics for air plants, and besides the array of wild orchids there are eleven species of bromeliad (plants livings off the air but usually attached to trees or other plants) and twenty species of fern growing there.

Florida black bear and Florida panther are found here, although there are not many of them. Also living in the Fakahatchee are raccoon, otter, and deer, as well as many wading birds during the dry season.

Although most of the old tram roads are overgrown, a few have been kept open by hunters, providing those who wish to visit this portion of the Big Cypress an ideal trail. At Sunniland are the remains of an old cypress mill, long since closed down. The sight of it brings back memories of the great exploitation of the Big Cypress during a time now passed into history.

Nearly every swamp in America—because of its fragile and delicate ecosystem—constantly faces danger of extinction, but the Big Cypress might well be labeled a classic example of an endangered swamp. Even though 570,000 acres were designated by Congress in 1974 as a National Water Preserve, the pressure of civilization upon the Big Cypress continues. And it has been that way for many years. The digging of canals into the swamp has shut off much of the water supply to the Florida Everglades and to the estuaries of the Ten Thousand Islands area, which was a great breeding ground for various marine creatures including the pink shrimp. Perhaps only when the last parcel of land is purchased by the Department of the Interior and additional stringent regulations are imposed limiting development in adjacent areas of the Big Cypress will the damage be reversed.

Although the Big Cypress represents an area of roughly 2,450 square miles, it is difficult to find a place within it where there are no reminders of man's presence. Litter abounds throughout much of the Big Cypress; hunting and fishing shacks were built in places so remote one wonders how its occupants were ever able to reach them. But the airboat and swamp buggy have made travel anywhere in the swamp feasible.

The most critical hour for the swamp was not the drainage of some of its territory, nor even running a toll road across its midst from Fort Lauderdale to Naples, it was in the 1970s when Miami was looking for a place to install a jetport. Like the airports of New York, Miami International was feeling the need for expansion and—like the Great Swamp of New Jersey—the Big Cypress seemed the logical place to do it. Bitter battles by environmentalists and conservationists have stopped that move, at least for the time being.

Despite man's exploitation of the Big Cypress, it remains a special kind of place. Once all the land is acquired by 1980 by the Department of the Interior through the National Park Service, it will likely begin within a few years to reclaim itself, for life here, while delicate, is also lush. During the rainy season and hot days, the Big Cypress becomes a jungle. Unlike the Everglades, the Big Cypress is largely dependent upon its own water resources, not those coming from outside its boundaries. And if those resources are tapped no further, the Big Cypress has a greater chance of survival than the Glades. Hunting will still be allowed, and many of those who have homes or camps in the swamp built before the congressional action will be allowed to keep them throughout their own lifetimes. But ultimately—as man relinquishes his

18. The yellow catopsis, one of the plants native to the Big Cypress, grows to a height of several feet. This one is about to bloom.

19. This tiny amber snail measures less than an inch long and is found deep in the strands of the Big Cypress and Corkscrew.

20. The tall plant with pointed leaves grows in deep water and is known as alligator flag. Alligator hunters traveling through the swamp used to look for this plant to tell them the whereabouts of deep holes where they might find alligators.

21. Wood storks dine at a Big Cypress waterhole with roseate spoonbills and immature white ibis (the bird with the

18

20

19

long curved beak). The roseate spoonbill normally feeds on shrimp in the salt-water portions of the Everglades, and there its plumage takes on a deep pink hue—thus its name. But a fresh-water diet causes the plumage to change to white with only a hint of pink.

21

hold and nature's inhabitants renew their grasp—the Big Cypress may again become an important natural area in south Florida.

Corkscrew Sanctuary. Near the northern tip of Florida's Big Cypress Swamp is the crown jewel of America's cypress swamps—Corkscrew Sanctuary. Geographically it is actually a part of the Big Cypress, but because of efforts of the National Audubon Society and lovers of nature everywhere, who endowed time and funds to salvage it during an eleventh-hour campaign, it has become more generally known as Corkscrew Sanctuary. Perhaps it is more appropriate that it should be so.

Containing some 11,000 acres and the nation's largest remaining stand of virgin bald cypress, Corkscrew is a refreshing interlude among swamps. Although it is small—compared to other major swamps generally—it is an example of what a cypress swamp should and would be, had man not interfered. Some of its cypress trees tower 140 feet above the swamp floor and are more than 700 years old.

Corkscrew became an Audubon Society sanctuary in 1954 after the formation of the Corkscrew Cypress Rookery Association. This particular place had long been a major rookery for wood stork and great egret, and it was for these as well as the virgin cypress that Corkscrew was eventually preserved.

A nationwide campaign was inaugurated by the National Audubon Society to raise funds, and soon more than $170,000 in contributions had been raised. The association purchased 2,240 acres from the Lee Tidewater Cypress Company and Collier Enterprises, both of which were sympathetic to their movement. In fact, had it not been for the attitude of these two large owners plus their willingness to make substantial contributions of additional acreage as a buffer zone around Corkscrew, the sanctuary would likely never have become a reality. Actually, it was because of the concern and conservation measures of these companies that the giant cypress had been spared from earlier timber cuttings. It was not so much out of consideration for the great trees as for the bird rookery they provided.

Thus Corkscrew was salvaged from future development. The swamp stands in black water that moves slowly, almost imperceptibly, down toward the Gulf of Mexico. Although the movement is hardly noticeable, giving the impression of stagnation, the water here is actually pure enough to drink during most of the year without ill effect.

Periodically, as you walk along the great circle boardwalk through the heart of Corkscrew, the swamp opens up into a meadow of water lettuce carpeting the surface of black-water lakes. These bodies of water, known locally as lettuce lakes, range from a few inches deep during the winter and spring dry season to as much as four feet deep in the year when the "monsoons" of south Florida begin. The lettuce lakes are part of the story of the evolution of the swamp. Only a hundred years ago, these same lakes were clear bodies of water, but now they are in the process of filling up. Ultimately, partially because of the vegetation growing upon them, they will become

131

muck and rich organic peat. Throughout the swamp are decaying logs of once giant trees. They too will contribute to the peat and build soil, thereby raising the elevation of the swamp until finally it is no longer swamp at all, but dry land. The process, however, is one that takes thousands of years.

The lakes play an important role in the present ecology of the swamp, for they are the reservoirs upon which the plants and wildlife must draw during drought periods. As the water level diminishes elsewhere, the plants die to be propagated again from seeds and spreading roots of their sister plants living in and around these fresh-water lakes. Wildlife congregates here, and this part of the cycle is the best time to visit Corkscrew.

During prolonged dry seasons or after frost, which occurs rarely this far south, the lettuce dies, sinking to the bottom to become a part of the muck floor of the lake. Although it is called lettuce, its resemblance to the garden variety is purely cosmetic. No one who has tried to eat the swamp variety would recommend it.

In many of the open areas, one is likely to see white ibis, the common egret, little blue heron, great blue, green heron, and the wood stork, the only stork species in North America.

The storks build their nests, lay their eggs, hatch and raise their young in the very tops of the virgin stand of cypress trees, but in plain view during the winter season of visitors on the boardwalks below. During the period—December to February—the wood stork, sometimes called the wood ibis, is the featured attraction for visitors to Corkscrew.

While many of the large birds, including the snowy egret and white ibis, were killed by the thousands by plume hunters over a period of many years, the wood stork, its coarse feathers less suitable for use, was not among them. Their population decline resulted instead from a gradual loss of feeding areas. Since 1939, the decline of feeding areas has been on the order of 90 percent.

If you venture into the swamp at night with a flashlight (you must obtain permission to do so), you often can detect the gleaming eyes of alligators on the prowl for food, for they are nocturnal feeders. Also, you'll find here those big spread-out spiders which live on the trunks of trees and, along the edges of water, a small dun-colored crayfish. The sanctuary is also home to the Florida mud turtle and the striped mud turtle, as well as the chicken turtle and red-bellied turtle. The latter two, particularly, may become part of the diet of the alligator, but his principle food supply is the garfish which breeds in profusion in the deeper pools of these waters.

After the land for Corkscrew was purchased, the National Audubon Society felt it had cleared all major hurdles. But new problems are constantly arising, many of them instigated by development of the lands upstate or in close proximity to the sanctuary. In the 1960s, for instance, additional land had to be added to preserve the integrity of the swamp. Audubon didn't have the funds but a generous grant by the Ford Foundation and hundreds of individual gifts enabled Audubon in 1968 to purchase

another 4,320 acres located south and north of the original holdings and to construct an impoundment which would prevent the swamp from drying out and dying.

Supt. Jerry Cutlip says further purchases may be necessary if the sanctuary is to survive, but he admits the future is much brighter today than it was in 1965.

Corkscrew Swamp is a remote outpost of wilderness in southern Florida. Its beauty is haunting and somewhat saddening, for one cannot forget that this isolated, perfect swamp is what all of the Florida Big Cypress would doubtless be had man not interfered with the course of nature.

22

23

24

22 and 23. *Thornbugs give the
appearance of thorns on the limbs
of this* Lysiloma *tree; thus their name.
Since they rarely move, many
visitors to the area believe them to be
actually a part of the tree.*

24. *During the summer and
fall rainy season, these logs
would be inundated with water; but by
January, all the water has virtually
disappeared in the black, spongy peat
soil.*

25. *This water snake lies beside a
pool waiting for mosquito fish,
chased by other fish in the water,
to leap virtually into his mouth,
saving him the effort of giving chase.*

25

CHAPTER
14
Mingo Swamp

Each generation has its own
rendezvous with the land, for
despite our fee titles and claims of ownership,
we are all brief tenants on this planet.
By choice or by default,
we carve out a land legacy for our heirs.

—Stewart Udall

In a sprawling depression created by an ancient river channel of the Mississippi in southeastern Missouri's boot-heel country is the swamp of the migrant birds—they call it Mingo. It's the only known swamp in America which lies across a major fault in the earth—the New Madrid fault.

While the origin of the name Mingo is uncertain, the most popular theory is that this swamp was named after Chief Mingo of the Shawnee who once lived nearby. The Indians sometimes referred to it as Black Mingo because of the dark waters and forbidding atmosphere. No Indians actually lived in the swamp, but several tribes came there to hunt, among them the Osage from the Southwest and the Shawnee who wandered down the Ohio and Mississippi.

Breaking the relatively flat terrain of the swamp are numerous ridges—folds in the earth—which may represent old sandbars or islands in the ancient bed of the Mississippi River. To the west lie the foothills of the Ozarks, while on the east the swamp is bordered by Crowley's Ridge.

Geologists say it was nearly a million years ago when the Mississippi River cut a deeply entrenched channel through this section. Over the years and with subsequent flooding, this entrenched valley was filled with alluvial soil deposited as silt, sand, and gravel from the river. Over a span of many years—until some 18,000 years ago—the river continued to build land in this portion until it became so choked there was no longer space for water flow. It was at this stage that the Mississippi sought an easier route south and shifted its course, leaving Mingo Swamp. Were it not for man's interference, the Mississippi likely would accomplish a similar feat with the Atchafalaya in Louisiana.

The lower end of the channel was choked with silt, allowing virtually no escape for drainage water collecting in the old channel. Consequently, it became first a swamp lake which attracted thousands of migrating waterfowl from the Mississippi flyway. In fall, the skies were darkened by Canada and snow geese, mallards and pintails, redheads and canvasbacks. Many of them spent the winter during mild seasons; they still do.

Today, Mingo Swamp, managed as a national wildlife refuge under the auspices of the Fish and Wildlife Service of the Department of the Interior since the mid-1940s, is a diverse haven for many species of wildlife, including otter, coyote, mink, and the swamp rabbit.

Biologically, the Mingo resembles the Big Thicket of Texas, for it, too, is a kind of crossroads. Many species of plants and fauna thriving here belong to different geological regions. It is, for instance, close to the northern range of the cottonmouth snake, the western perimeter of the copperhead. The swamp rabbit, which is endangered, is not found much farther north either, but wildlife biologists at Mingo believe one of the denser populations in the nation is found here.

The principle emphasis of the refuge, however, is not the protection of the swamp rabbit, but providing suitable habitat for migrating waterfowl. Fields adjacent to the swamp are sown in grain crops—rice, corn, and millet—

2

3

4

5

6

1 and 2. Persimmon trees grow throughout Mingo and, following the first good frost, provide excellent fruit for opossum and raccoon.

3. Many types of mushrooms grow in Mingo, but these oyster mushrooms are among the most common.

4. Cockspur hawthorn provide food for birds during the winter months and beauty for a drab winter landscape.

5. This growth, normally found on old decaying logs in wet areas, is commonly known as turkey-tail fungus.

6. A hornet's nest, a marvel in architectural design, clings on after its season's use is spent.

7. (Overleaf) Fog rising from the shallow pools of Mingo on an autumn morning give the swamp an eerie, brooding atmosphere.

8. Numerous mosses and wood sorrel may be found in Mingo, many growing around decaying logs.

9. This manmade impoundment at Mingo is one of two major ones provided for migrating waterfowl.

10. The swamp is quiet as evening approaches, but in the early hours of the morning, it will be alive with the sounds of thousands of feeding ducks and geese.

8

9

which are harvested by the geese and ducks during the fall and winter. The swamp is fed by overflows from the Castor and St. Francis Rivers, but impoundments are manipulated by the Fish and Wildlife Service to offer feeding areas. On alternate years impoundments are drained to allow plant growth and then are reflooded. The draining causes more verdant aquatic growth beneficial to waterfowl. From the time the snows begin to fly in Minnesota and Wisconsin, until March or April, the honk of the wild goose is a familiar sound at Mingo.

Boardwalks have been provided in a couple of spots along the single drive open to the public so one may park his automobile and walk into the swamp to blinds and observation points to watch the wildlife at close range. The best time to go, says Refuge Manager Gerry Clawson, is just after dawn or just before sunset, when the greatest feeding activity occurs. Fishermen and hunters come to the swamp in certain seasons—the fishermen in quest of buffalo, largemouth bass, crappie, catfish, and bream; the hunters for deer or squirrel.

Covering some 16,000 acres of the 21,673-acre refuge, the swamp is, like many of America's swamps now preserved, slowly recovering from abuse at the hands of man. There are grim reminders still to be seen. Drainage ditches bisect the area, and atop the dirt removed from them roads or trails were built which are being utilized to this day. For two years—around 1918–20—extensive efforts were made to drain the swamp for the purposes of agriculture. Land was cleared of all growth, and wildfires repeatedly burned over the area. The black cypress lands were cleared for farming while homes were built on the sand knolls and ridges in the swamp.

The farming on the lowlands and alluvial fans was primarily based on corn. This one-crop type of farming rapidly eroded and depleted the soil. Coupled with only partially successful drainage, this caused many crop failures, and ultimately the landowners began to look elsewhere. The swamp didn't seem such a great place to farm after all. Those who remained tried running hogs throughout the swamp to feed upon the acorns and persimmons. Following a few years of such treatment, there was very little in the swamp that could be associated with wilderness. All the understory was gone, most of the giant trees had been felled, the area burned, tilled, leached, and left to itself. But with more than forty inches of rainfall each year and a long growing season, the swamp quickly recovered. It will be years yet before it will begin to appear as it once did, but at least it's moving in that direction. Among the trees now on the refuge are fifteen state and two national champions.

Some 1,700 acres of the swamps refuge already have been set aside to be preserved as wilderness. Called the Black Mingo Wilderness Area, no engines are allowed here; man must enter on foot or by canoe via the Black Mingo River. But it's in this section one is most apt to find some of the rarer species of the swamp—the white-tailed deer, the bobcat, the coyote, the wild turkey. It takes stealth and silence and a good sense of woodsmanship, of the sort practiced by the Indians who once hunted here.

11

11. *A spider huddles near the center of its dew-drenched web, patiently awaiting its prey.*

12. *Sloughs drain off excess water accumulating in the swamp.*

13. *The swamp rabbit, called "swamper" by local folks, is found in greater concentration at Mingo Swamp than at any other spot along the Mississippi Valley.*

14. *Bobcat roam freely in many sections of the swamp.*

13

14

CHAPTER
15
The Atchafalaya

Over their heads the towering and tenebrous boughs
    of the cypress
Met in a dusky arch, and trailing mosses in mid-air
Waved like banners that hang on the walls of ancient
    cathedrals.

        —Henry Wadsworth Longfellow *Evangeline*

Along Louisiana's bayou country near the Mississippi Delta lies the third largest swamp in America—the Atchafalaya. Some of the local people call it the swamp on the move. With the exception of a 23,000-acre state-owned wildlife management area in the vicinity of Grand Lake, virtually none of it has been preserved for posterity.

The Atchafalaya (pronounced locally Sha-fa-LI) takes its name from the Atchafalaya River, a distributary of the Mississippi, which provides a shortcut to the Gulf of Mexico. The name Atchafalaya, which means "long river," came from the Chitimachas Indians. It actually isn't a long river, extending from just south of the confluence of the Red with the Mississippi to the marshy delta on the Gulf, a distance of only about 140 miles. But to the Chitimachas, who traveled on foot or in shallow cypress dugouts, forerunners of the Cajun pirogues, that represented many days of walking or paddling. To them, it *was* a long river.

Along both sides of the meandering river lies the floodplain swamp, seventeen miles wide at its narrowest point, a mysterious mixture that is neither land or water but a composite of both. For more than a hundred miles, it sprawls north and south, 860,000 acres fed and kept alive by muddy overflow waters from the river.

The swamp was an Eden to the Chitimachas long before the pioneer came this way, for they liked what they saw here. Many settled along the shorelines of the river and on the ridges of the basin. The fertile land, many species of fish, and an abundance of game provided them with a good livelihood. In fact, a number of Indian tribes used the Atchafalaya during the early days of Louisiana history. It was their crossroads on endless searches for new home sites. Many were agriculturists, and this would have been ideal territory for them, but because of conflicts and increasing exploits by the Spanish, the French, and later westward expansion from the colonies, most of them soon moved westward.

Today, thousands of fishermen come to the Atchafalaya year-round to angle the waters for largemouth bass, catfish, bream, and sac-a-lait (white crappie). Crawfish, considered a delicacy in Cajun country, breed profusely all along the many bayous that compose the Atchafalaya; and families come for miles—from New Orleans to Houston—in the late winter and spring in search of them. As one Cajun lady put it: "This is gumbo heaven."

The Atchafalaya is home for more than the crawfish, however. As I canoed one October Saturday through the oil fields of Henderson Lake just north of Interstate 10 (the only major highway to cross the swamp) my craft slithered past the coiled shapes of cottonmouth moccasins sunning on cypress stumps left from a cutting forty years ago. An anhinga (some call them water turkeys or snake birds) perched with outstretched wings to dry on a skeleton tree that spread its limbs above dark water. It was a peaceful place, once you piloted your canoe out of earshot of the humming traffic on the interstate. You could become lost here in this forested lake and enjoy it, at least until nightfall when droves of mosquitoes would come out of the woods and eat you alive.

The Atchafalaya, from purely an economic standpoint,

1

Louisiana Highway Commission

2

1. *A few years ago these spits of land were not here, and during high water, when the Mississippi and Atchafalaya rivers flood, you can't see them. Next year, they will be an inch or two higher. As the silt settles, the movements of water cause it to form ridges. Trees then grow upon them and keep them intact.*

2. *Interstate 10 was built across the Atchafalaya; even the floods do not affect it.*

3. *The remote backwaters of the Atchafalaya resemble a Louisiana bayou.*

is one of the most productive swamps in America. In 1975, for instance, nearly $200-million worth of oil and gas was pumped from the swamp, $100,000 worth of timber was harvested, and commercial fishing produced more than $2.5 million. Trapping of fur-bearing animals such as muskrat and nutria produced another $1 million.

Although the state of Louisiana has made some headway in opening part of the Atchafalaya to the public, most of the swamp is owned either by timber or oil companies. While there's little timber left to harvest, they hope there will be again someday, and therefore they hold on to their lands, posting most of them against trespassers. The sportsmen resent this, of course, and are bringing pressure to bear upon political forces in the state to open the swamp to the public.

The canoe is an ideal craft, as is the pirogue, for maneuvering the bayous, for it will operate in shallow water, can be easily turned, and fits well in narrow places. Many of the bayous are choked with water hyacinths three-quarters of the year (they die back in the winter), presenting a problem that has plagued government agencies and others in attempting to control them. They're beautiful, however, particularly when they carpet the water with feathery lavender blooms.

The Atchafalaya River, in essence, is an escape valve which siphons off the floodwaters of the Mississippi, eliminating potential damage to such populated areas as Baton Rouge and New Orleans. The Mississippi floods the Atchafalaya River which, in turn, floods the swamp.

But the Atchafalaya River has proven itself to be more than a theoretical escape valve. At one time, it nearly took matters into its own hands and stole the Mississippi. Had it not been for some efforts on the part of the U.S. Army Corps of Engineers, the Atchafalaya, because it supplied a shorter and straighter route to the sea, likely would have diverted the entire flow of the Great River from a point near the Louisiana-Mississippi border, channeling it a hundred or so miles west of New Orleans. That would have meant economic disaster to both Baton Rouge and New Orleans, since both cities depend heavily upon world shipping. So the corps, under great political pressure, had to act fast.

To avert this dramatic change, the engineers built a lock and dam across the Old River which joins the Mississippi to the Atchafalaya. In this way, the flow of water could be regulated and, at the same time, allow navigation. But the Atchafalaya still isn't under control. Each time there is serious flooding, smaller towns along the Atchafalaya suffer huge damage and sometimes loss of life. And the corps, which expects the worst, is planning its operations around expectations for a great flood—greater than any known in the history of this country—which they say occurs about every 340 years.

To protect the area from the "project flood," the corps spent millions of taxpayers' dollars in construction of levees and millions more in maintaining them along the Atchafalaya Basin. Not many people objected to that, but when the corps decided the Atchafalaya River needed dredging and channelization, a project which would have left the adjacent swampland dry except perhaps during that

3

147

4. *The Atchafalaya is one of the most commercial swamps in America; oil tanks and a pumping station in the background are part of that commerce.*

5. *Henderson Lake.*

6. *A cluster of cypress knees protrude from the waters of the swamp. Their function is unclear to botanists.*

7. *At the turn of the century, these cypress trees were standing and green; today they are merely tall stumps, probably cut by crews in boats when the water was high.*

4

6

7

big flood that happens along every 340 years, the sportsmen and environmentalists arose en masse. To restrict the Atchafalaya with levees was one thing; to eliminate it altogether was quite another. The corps began their project on the upper end of the basin where the populace was more agriculturally minded and thus more friendly to such a project.

The corps didn't buy the land in the project. Instead, it bought flood easements over the land, many of them at full fee value. The landowners kept the title, and the corps, having paid for the land, proceeded to dry it out so that landowners could farm it. Why shouldn't the landowners be friendly toward the idea? They were getting something for nothing. West of the river, owners even began to build houses and move their farm headquarters to locations within the basin, behind those same levees that hopefully would contain the great flood.

When the corps's action became known, many Louisianans became greatly concerned. They banded together and tried, sometimes successfully, to get the corps to consider wildlife values, to leave a few bayous open. But the dredging project moved on. The heavy machinery was working inexorably southward. Then, in the eleventh hour, help came from an unexpected quarter. The same Congress which had authorized the project passed the National Environmental Policy Act which required all federal agencies—even the corps—to consider the environmental effects of their actions, and alternative courses of action, before moving ahead on any project. Conservationists in the state saw this as their new opportunity to get something done. They solicited the support of such national organizations as the Audubon Society, the Sierra Club, the National Wildlife Federation, and others.

In 1971 the opposition became substantial enough that, after twelve months of operation, the corps agreed to halt their operations pending a public opinion survey and a comprehensive study of the environmental effects of its action, as well as all possible alternative courses of action. Meanwhile, the corps still pushed for support of its project, for it figured channelization would solve the problem of flooding and the environmentalists would soon forget anyway.

The Atchafalaya, however, may be more complex than even the corps believes. For with or without the help of the corps, the swamp seems destined for change, perhaps annihilation.

Each time the Atchafalaya floods and spills into the Atchafalaya Basin, the waters bring with them heavy silt. As the current slows in the Atchafalaya, the silt naturally settles to the bottom which, in turn, builds land. Since the heaviest silting occurs in the upper Atchafalaya, it's natural that land elevations form there at a faster pace than anywhere else, so fast, in fact, that much of the upper end of what once was swamp is now dry farmland.

The silting, however, is having a dramatic effect along the entire Atchafalaya Swamp. In the lower end, for instance, lakes and tidal ponds where the fresh water is mixed with the salt water of the Gulf when the two meet are being eliminated. More and more earth fills in the lakes, and the delta extends farther and farther into the Gulf of Mexico.

The problem really begins far upstream in heartland America, however. Because erosion from the farmlands (the Mississippi drainage covers all or parts of thirty-one states and two Canadian provinces) increases each year, the amount of silting in the Atchafalaya also increases. The greater the erosion, the greater the silting.

Dr. Charles Fryling of Louisiana State University, who did special studies on the Atchafalaya Basin over a period of several years, labels the swamp unique in this respect, for here, he said, you can literally watch the death of a swamp as it evolves into dry land. Had the Corps of Engineers not tampered with the basin by building containing levees, hydrologists say the swamp might have regenerated itself by moving east or west into new territory as the high ground forced the water to other areas. But the levees restrict the flow of water, and now the levees must constantly be increased in height to stay one step ahead of the silting process.

Solutions may not be easy to find, regardless of whether the corps resumes its channelization project. Had the corps been allowed to continue its project, the Atchafalaya would undoubtedly have become farmland much sooner than it will at the hands of nature. Unless some unknown factor can be brought to bear, however, to eliminate the silting of the swamp, it may become developed land anyway.

Considering the fact that it will take nothing short of a miracle to save the Atchafalaya, efforts to save the swamp may be of questionable value. As a wilderness area, it certainly can and should be preserved from commercial exploitation. But unless erosion is curbed in all the area drained by the Mississippi, the silting of the Atchafalaya Basin is not likely to stop. As some hydrologists believe, the swamp may indeed only move southward, extending farther and farther into the Gulf delta country as it fills in on the north. But to try to maintain it in its present position might be compared to holding back the flow of the Mississippi with a hand shovel. Nature is likely to take its course regardless of the plans of the Corps of Engineers.

Many Louisianans—among them the Atchafalaya Basin Commission Director Sandra Thompson—consider the preservation of the swamp a top priority, but without cooperation from the federal government and from states upstream in meeting and resolving the problem of erosion, the Atchafalaya in its present position seems doomed.

8. Some of the great cypress trees in the Atchafalaya are hollow and stand on thin supports, but it may be twenty-five years before they succumb and fall into the swamp.

9

9. *A dragonfly rests on some vines in the swamp between pursuit of other flying insects such as mosquitoes and gnats. The largest modern dragonfly has a wing-span of about 7.5 inches, but dragonflies that lived 250 million years ago had wing-spans exceeding 2 feet, making them the largest insects that ever lived.*

10. *The soft lavender of water hyacinths in bloom adds beauty to the Atchafalaya.*

11. *Detail of water hyacinths.*

12. *The soft symmetry of cypress leaves. Their color indicates autumn, but in February the cypress begin to grow a new crop.*

10

13. *A little blue heron searches for fish in shallow water in the lower Atchafalaya.*

14. *A species of the rat snake which inhabits the Atchafalaya Swamp is shown here searching trees for birds' nests. They will not only eat eggs, but tiny birds as well, swallowing them whole.*

11

13

12

14

CHAPTER
16
The Everglades

The whole system was like a set of scales
on which the sun and the rains, the winds,
the hurricanes and the dewfalls, were balanced
so that the life of the vast grass
and all its . . . forms were kept secure.

—Marjory Stoneman Douglas
The Everglades

Across a sweeping expanse of south Florida lies one of the most unusual bodies of water in the world. For while the Everglades is loosely labeled a swamp, it is more appropriately a river, forty miles wide and three inches deep during the rainy season. During the dry season—roughly from December to May—the water flow is barely perceptible. But there must always be water, for without it the Everglades and its creatures cannot survive. Indians call this strange river Pa-Hay-Okee, meaning simply "grassy water."

The vastness of the Everglades is overwhelming—13,000 square miles. Stand at any spot within its periphery and look about you. It seems to extend forever in every direction, and the only sound to be heard is the moan of the trade winds in the sawgrass. The plant and animal communities of the Everglades combine tropical and subtropical characteristics, and one can mark the climatic change by traveling from Lake Okeechobee down to Flamingo on Florida Bay. The upland forest changes to sawgrass prairies, punctuated by elevated tree islands, eventually giving way to a broad mangrove belt interlaced by a labyrinth of waterways lying along the Gulf Coast.

The story is told of a cowboy who, upon first sight of the Grand Canyon, exclaimed: "Something sure has happened here." If that same cowboy were to come to the Everglades, his conclusion might be that nothing has ever happened here. He would be wrong.

There is in fact no other place in America with greater diversity or drama than the Florida Everglades. It changes dramatically from the ecosystems found in the pinelands, which represent the highest ground in the Glades to the salt-water mangrove swamps along its southern and western perimeter. Actually the Glades seem to just fade from view into a mudflat dotted with keys in Florida Bay. During the rainy season, life is abundant; but as the dry season proceeds, the struggle for use of what water remains becomes dramatic and violent. It is then that great fires are most likely to sweep the land.

While early Spanish explorers apparently veered away from the Everglades, there were people living here long before America was discovered by Europeans. Historians say even the Seminole Indians were not the first to come here. The first are believed to have arrived about 15,000 years ago from Asia, part of the horde that crossed the Bering Strait from that continent to spread southward and eastward. The Calusa appear in south Florida history as the first strong tribe to emerge among those primitive Indians, about 2,000 years ago. They lived largely upon seafood, prowling the ocean shores and marshy Everglades salt rivers in their crude canoes.

Later, of course, came the Seminoles, driven into the Glades by white soldiers from their lands in northern Florida and in the Okefenokee Swamp. But they were not known as Seminoles until 1775 when the Americans engaged in the Revolutionary War with England. In the Indian dialect from which the name is derived, Seminole means a people who choose to be free. The name was used by the Colonists, however, to brand these Indians as renegades and deserters.

During the bitter Seminole Wars of 1835–42, the In-

1

2

3

1. *A sweeping view of the Everglades, a river of sawgrass, sometimes called a prairie.*

2. *Wood stork, common egret, and white ibis often feed together among the sawgrass.*

3. *The upper Glades, late in the dry season. In the wet season, this landscape will become a river of shallow water except for the dark-colored tree islands.*

4

Lee Jenkins

5

6

7

8

9

4. *The southern bullfrog is one of several species found in the Glades.*

5. *These huge lubber grasshoppers may become as large as five inches long, and are so vile tasting that virtually nothing will eat them.*

6. *The American anole, or chameleon, as it is more commonly known, changes colors to blend in with its surroundings. These gentle creatures are among the most fascinating found in the swamp, for you can actually watch them change from a rustic brown to a brilliant green in a matter of moments.*

7. *A pair of white ibis in the mangrove jungle portion of the Everglades. Immature ibis look much the same, but have brown feathers.*

8. *Many of the deeper pools in the Glades produce an aquatic plant called pondweed. Fish use it as protective cover against other predators.*

9. *A mockingbird.*

10

11

10. *When the anhinga comes out of the water, it must first preen its feathers and dry them in the wind before it can fly. To allow its feathers to dry, the anhinga spreads its wings and sits sometimes for hours.*

11. *Known also as the water turkey or snake bird, you can see the resemblance to each in this shot. Note the spread, submerged tail feathers as the bird swims. The head sticking up above the water, some say, resembles a snake. The anhinga swims underwater, emerging only for air. It stabs fish under water, surfaces to toss them into the air and swallows them head first.*

12. *The male anhinga (shown here) is black with a sprinkling of white in its wings. The female anhinga has brown on the neck.*

13. *(Overleaf) White ibis and common egret winging their way over the Glades.*

12

dians fought with a ferocity that startled the world. They became the only Indians the U.S. never managed to defeat completely, although the army tried very hard. In 1823, thirty-two of the Seminole chiefs reluctantly signed the Treaty of Moultrie Creek, in which they agreed to occupy assigned lands as their reservation. But the Indians had little faith in such an agreement, for treaty after treaty had been broken by the whites, as were subsequent treaties, and the Seminoles have, even as late as World War II, come nearly to the brink of war with the United States. The Seminoles have been the most constant tenants of the Everglades and Big Cypress swamps, but theirs has not been the only influence. Before the turn of the century, plume hunters started coming into the Everglades to shoot the egrets and herons. Their plumage was in great demand for ladies' hats, and many conflicts—even murders—occurred between plume hunters and federal agents and state game wardens attempting to stop the massacre. Despite this, considerable numbers of large birds, as well as other wildlife, remain to this day.

At no other spot in all of this country is there a greater concentration or variety of wildlife than in the Glades, yet you must look carefully to see much of it. The Everglades is a place of seclusion and obscurity. Many of its residents are rare; some, such as the crocodile, are found nowhere else in North America.

If one looks closely at the Everglades today, one sees signs of change, perhaps, to take a dark view, signs of death. One of the first indicators of ecological change are the birds, primarily because they are highly mobile and visible. If an area does not provide them with their needs, they simply won't come there. And the birds no longer come to the Everglades in the great numbers of other days. In 1945, at the end of World War II, 1.5 million wading birds nested in what is now the Everglades National Park. In 1975, just thirty years later, fewer than 50,000 large wading birds nested there, a reduction of 1,450,000 birds.

During the winter of 1974–75, few large wading birds were seen south of the Tamiami Trail. National Park Service officials speculated it might be because food was more plentiful elsewhere than it had been in previous years. But perhaps it was instead that the birds sensed, as wildlife often senses strange phenomena, the coming change in the southern part of the Everglades; for the lack of fresh water and the influx of salt water is indeed already changing the life-support systems of the southern Everglades.

In fact, the Everglades is constantly changing. Some of those changes are hardly noticeable; others—such as the great fires that march across the swamp near the end of the dry season—are spectacular.

On the southern end of the Everglades, the mangrove is helping to build new land to add to the swamp. It would take a billion years to see substantial difference, but the land-building process is going on constantly just the same. First a single mangrove plant may spring forth from the shallow mudflats. Then another. And ultimately there will be others until there is a forest of mangrove. Land begins to fill in, washed there by the tides and trapped by the roots. Within a few years mangrove islands begin to form

161

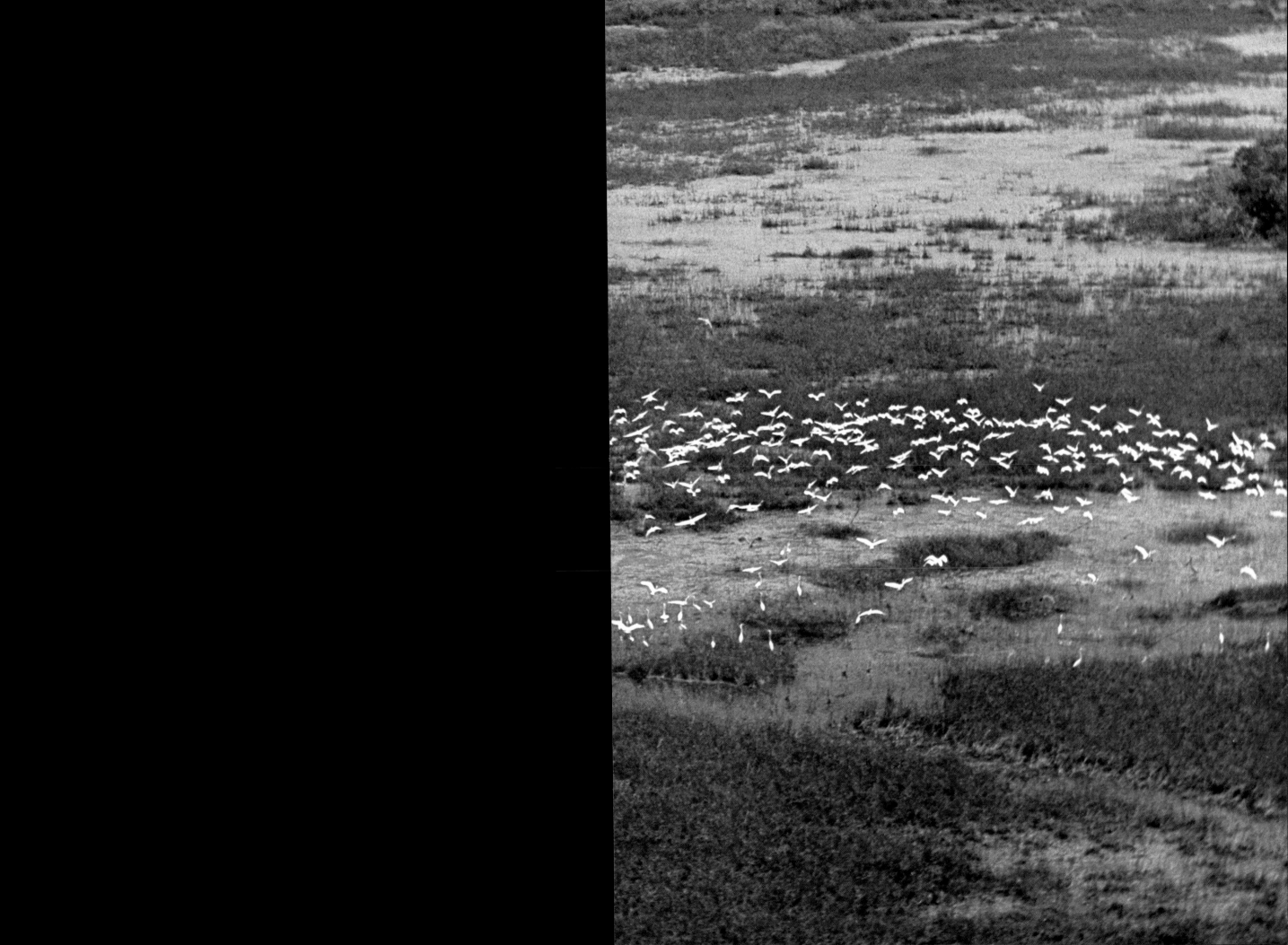

(they are locally called keys). New islands form and sandbars and mudflats between them until eventually, geologists feel, there will be new additions to the Glades. But that is millennia away.

Late in the winter, under normal conditions, there are birds everywhere in the Glades. At few other places in the world are there greater opportunities for bird-watching, especially for large wading birds—the herons, egrets, and ibis. Snake birds and bald eagles and the roseate spoonbill, the latter resembling some prehistoric leftover—all call this home. The Everglades is to wildlife what New York City is to ethnic groups—a melting pot.

The geological foundation of the Everglades is a feature known as the Floridian Plateau, some 300 miles wide. Made up of volcanic and altered rocks, it is largely permeable and would allow water to rapidly soak into its depths. This permeable limestone core is covered with a rock that is impermeable—marl. Laid down as sediment by an ancient sea, marl strongly resembles coral, but is actually Miami oolite (limestone). Its jagged edges can be seen protruding from the ground in many places throughout the Everglades. During the winter, they lie barren in the hot sun; in summer, they are often inundated by shallow flows of water which deposit decaying matter in the crevices of the rocks, thereby increasing the Glades's ability to produce new plant life and at the same time calking any crevices that might drink up the life-giving waters as they flow southward to the sea.

The Glades has no hills; its terrain is nearly at sea level. At no spot in southern Florida is the elevation more than ten feet above sea level, but the tilt of the earth is just enough to provide a constant if subtle drainage. The average seaward slope is no more than a few inches per mile, and so runoff is slow. It is this stagnant or slow-moving water that allows us to classify the Everglades as a swamp.

Rainfall in this area averages about sixty inches a year, and there have been occasional floods. The ones, which caused the greatest loss of life and property damage, occurred in 1926 and again in 1928 when hurricanes created giant waves on Lake Okeechobee. To control these floods, the Army Corps of Engineers has slashed canals leading from Lake Okeechobee out to sea. They have also built a levee on the banks of the lake to keep it from spilling.

The natural course of overflow from Lake Okeechobee is down the River of Grass some seventy-five to eighty miles through the Everglades. With this flow largely diverted, it is now controlled by man through various water districts established for water management in south Florida. The system is rather complex and has never worked according to plan or promise. Today water shortage is a critical factor in the Everglades, and during dry years, its waterholes have dried up, its wildlife perished. Regardless of what changes are made at the water control level, the Everglades will never again be exactly what it was before the dikes and canals were built. Nor will there likely ever again be the great concentration of wildlife that once existed there.

The upper Glades supported much more fertile soil at greater depth than the lower, so it was natural that early

14. *A little blue heron scans the water for fish.*

15. *A common egret.*

16. *A brown pelican on the water at Flamingo where the Everglades meets the Bay of Florida.*

15

16

17. *A gator floats silently and motionless, waiting for unsuspecting prey to come within easy reach.*

18, 19 and 20. *The liguus tree snail, implanted, it's thought, by hurricanes from the West Indies, comes in fifty-two color varieties, of which three are shown here. The liguus tree snail is normally found only on smooth-barked trees such as the* Lysiloma *or gumbo limbo.*

21. *The harmless yellow rat snake is one of the most colorful and gentle reptiles of the Everglades.*

22. *Alligator flag, so called because it grows only in deep water, usually an alligator hole.*

17

18

19

20

21

22

settlers in the area began thinking about what great crops they might raise upon it if the swamp were drained. And in 1906, aided by incompetent state officials, they began to drain it. Promoters moved into the area and began billing it as "black gold." That it was, for the rich earth combined with bountiful rainfall and long days of hot sunshine year-round, brought forth miraculous crops. Much of the area was planted in sugar cane, and today it is one of the richest sugar cane-producing areas in the nation.

The demand for more drained land compressed the Everglades into a smaller and smaller area. Had the depth of topsoil been adequate to produce agricultural crops all the way south to Florida Bay, it too would quite probably have become farmland. But it was not, so pressure there was not as great.

The lower Glades might have turned into something else—condominiums or housing developments—had not the state of Florida and U.S. Department of the Interior moved to preserve the Everglades. Part of the Glades was established as a national wildlife refuge—the Loxahatchee—and part of it was given to the Miccosukee Indians to be administered by them and the Bureau of Indian Affairs. Some was turned over to commercial interests and farmland. But 1.4 million acres were set aside as the Everglades National Park. And next door, in 1974, the Big Cypress National Fresh Water Preserve was authorized by Congress.

In 1965 when the park was about to be destroyed for lack of water, conservationists nationwide rose up to demand that the Flood Control District spare the park. And only after weeks of static from the citizenry did the state agency reluctantly, and briefly, open one of its four Tamiami Trail spillways that feed this national park portion of the Everglades. For one week, the district opened the gate just one inch. The help this gave the huge, dying Everglades National Park, one irate conservationist said, was like spitting on a forest fire.

The lack of adequate fresh water in the Everglades is having dire effects which are often overlooked by those who do not live in the area. Only the pressure of fresh water keeps back the intrusion of salt water. Somewhere in the lower Everglades National Park, this mingling of salt water with fresh occurs, and the demarcation line changes as fresh-water supplies fluctuate. When there's not as much fresh water coming through the park, naturally the salt water rushes in and the brackish water is found further inland than it was previously.

Not only does this hold true for the park, but it also holds true for the subterranean water in all of south Florida. There have been many instances in the Miami area, for example, in the 1970s where fresh-water wells tapped into the Floridian aquifer have overnight become salty. The transition could conceivably occur in all of south Florida. The Corps of Engineers, never at a loss for ingenious, complicated schemes, has a solution for that situation, however. If all of south Florida water becomes saline, the corps could tap the Suwannee River, which flows into the Gulf of Mexico in the northern part of the state, and divert it to Miami. This ultimately might have some drainage effect upon the Okefenokee Swamp, especially if the

167

23. *The purple gallinule, one of the shyest and most difficult-to-photograph birds in the Everglades. Note the huge feet designed for walking upon the spatterdock.*

24. *Salt-water birds, mostly plovers and skimmers, gather over the mudflats along the mangrove swamp when the tide is out.*

25. *The Gulf fritillary butterfly.*

26. *The interior of the hammocks or tree islands in the Glades is a dense and dark jungle.*

27. *The long-legged flamingo dwarf the fulvous tree duck. Each species is rare in the Everglades.*

28. *The zebra butterfly is one of the few tropical creatures to occupy the Everglades. Note the shape of the wings as compared with the wings of other butterflies you've seen.*

29. *A great wood stork (some of them have a four-foot wing-span) takes to the air.*

23

25

26

28

29

27

30

31

demand were serious enough that it forced water out of the river more quickly than the swamp could supply it.

The National Audubon Society charged in 1965: ". . . there is a shortage in southern Florida not of water but of clear-headed ways to prevent its enormous waste." It further charged: "Because of unbelievable bungling, the managers of the flood control project that borders the park dump more water into the sea in one season than the park could use in years." And the *New York Times* added: "The Everglades have been seriously damaged by the Army Engineers. Neither the greed of Florida land promoters nor the bureaucratic arrogance of the Corps of Engineers can be allowed to place the Everglades in danger of extinction."

Immediately following these charges, unusually heavy rains inundated the Glades and drowned many of its mammals. The Flood Control District could have held the water back, but, irritated at the criticisms leveled the year before, it allowed the other extreme to occur in the Glades.

Subsequent droughts have developed in the Everglades, and it has burned time and time again in areas where fire is not needed, destroying much valuable wildlife habitat. Even while it burned, the Corps of Engineers was digging a canal from the Atlantic Ocean near Homestead, Fla., to accommodate an Aerojet General Corporation plant (built to conduct solid-fuel rocket motor tests) so that shipping of rocket motors and supplies could conveniently be barged to the plant's front door. This project would have drained more fresh water from the Glades and perhaps allowed an influx of salt water. It cost the taxpayers millions of dollars, and when the last plug of earth was about to be removed, despite objections by the National Park Service and the Audubon Society that the Everglades might be destroyed forever by salt water, the corps was still planning to go ahead. Only when legal action was threatened by then Park Service Director George B. Hartzog did the corps pause. The canal has not been opened, but it remains an ominous threat to the Everglades. Any time concerned people look the other way, the plug could be pulled.

The northern part of the Everglades faces a different, even more serious crisis—one that is again related to water, but may also involve weather and climate. Dr. Arthur Marshall, formerly of the University of Miami's Division of Applied Ecology, claims the construction of canals and the resulting loss of water from Lake Okeechobee has resulted in the drying out of the muck which acts as a giant sponge in the upper portion of the Glades. The muck retains water during the wet season and slowly releases it in the dry season.

The muck was formed as the result of summer flooding and related growth of vegetation, but during the forty-year period since the upper Glades was first drained, more than five feet of muck have been destroyed. Dr. Marshall claims that within another twenty-five years the muck will disappear entirely in the Lake Okeechobee agricultural area, and perhaps sooner if the muck catches fire. Then there will no longer be any soil, but instead only sharply eroded pinnacle rock. Dr. Marshall believes the disappearance of the muck, based upon the theory that drought induces drought, could change climatic conditions in south Florida.

Marshall has come up with a plan for reversing the trends in south Florida, for preserving the Everglades and its wildlife. So have others. None had actually been put into effect by 1975. The Everglades is in grave danger, and as Dr. Marshall has pointed out, when the Everglades goes, the rest of south Florida is likely to follow soon.

32

30. Wading birds and ducks at a waterhole in the south Glades.

31. A Louisiana heron feeds in the Shark Valley portion of Everglades National Park.

32. Roseate spoonbills, so named because of their spoonlike bill, and immature white ibis. The spoonbills shown here are pale in color because they have been feeding in fresh water.

33. *Fire is a necessary part of the ecology of the Everglades. Without it, certain species of plants and trees would soon be smothered out by quick-growing jungle species such as palmetto and sabal palm.*

34. *Sometimes the fires burn for days on end, and with the trade winds blowing constantly, there's practically no way to extinguish them.*

35. *As the fires burn to the end of day and into the night, rangers keep watch to forecast changes that may cause critical concern.*

36. *The fires normally come near the end of the dry winter season when the water has disappeared and the earth has become parched and cracked.*

37. *As the water disappears, the land settles leaving ridges of corallike marl rock exposed.*

38. *Once the fire has passed, there remains only the blackened and charred swamp floor. Within a few weeks, however, new growth will turn the earth green once again.*

33

34

35

36

37

38

39. *Black mangrove roots form an interesting array along the shoreline in the salt-water portion of the Everglades.*

40. *A cluster of red mangrove roots. Among these many small salt-water creatures take refuge.*

41. *A pygmy rattlesnake is poisonous, but usually has to be provoked into an attack.*

42 and 43. *Bleached cypress and mangrove trees, a reminder of the hurricanes that pass through the Everglades.*

44. *These mangrove shoots, growing in salt water, trap silt which will eventually form dry land.*

39

40

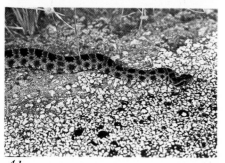

41

42

43

44

45. *(Overleaf) Sunset on the East Glades.*

CHAPTER
17
The Swamp Lakes

Wilderness is an anchor to windward.
Knowing it is there, we can also know that we
are still a rich nation . . .
—Senator Clinton P. Anderson

Straddled across the Texas-Louisiana border west of Shreveport is one of the most fascinating lakes in America. They call it Caddo. There are those who claim it was formed by an earthquake, but some oldtimers in the area have their own ideas. Wyatt Moore of Karneck, Texas, thinks it was due to the perennial flooding of the Red River out of Arkansas and log jams downstream that caused the river to spread out until it was so shallow it allowed cypress and other plant life to thrive. Over a period of years during which heavy silting occurred, the bottom of the lake rose to the point where it became a combination of swamp and lake.

Indeed there is evidence today the lake is in a state of transition. Rushes and cattails grow now where the water was too deep not so many years ago. And along ridges on the floor of the lakes densely populated by bald cypress and willow thrive carpets of water hyacinths, which grow profusely and spread rapidly, choking the waterways.

On the night of December 15, 1811, the New Madrid earthquake gave this continent its greatest shock in recorded history. That night—when fearful rumblings, hissings, and fissures inflicted tidal waves upon the shores of the bayous, and tremors were felt thousands of miles across the continent—is considered by geologists and historians to be the beginning of Caddo Lake.

Directly north some 300 miles, another lake—Reelfoot—was formed by that same earthquake in western Tennessee near the Kentucky border. At Reelfoot many members of the Chickasaw tribe perished as the Mississippi River actually flowed upstream, broke across country and filled a low-lying area, drowning all inhabitants.

The Caddo Indians, from whom the lake takes its name, fared somewhat better, however. According to an Indian legend still handed down among remnants of the Caddo tribe in Oklahoma, a chief of the tribe was forewarned by the Great Spirit of approaching disaster. Summoning the tribe, he led them to the safety of higher ground, believed to be what is now Caddo State Park on Cypress Bayou. The story is partially supported by archeological evidence, for Indian relics found since the turn of the century in shallow water near Big Green Brake indicated a large village there was abandoned in great haste and was never visited again. Historians and archeologists at the University of Texas believe that the Caddo legend, although colored through generations of repetition, is basically accurate.

Both Reelfoot and Caddo were, prior to the quake, depressed swamp areas, so the further sinking of the earth caused by the quake and the breakthrough of streams to feed those earth depressions quickly changed their physical character.

Today Caddo Lake is a fascinating wooded lake with pond cypress growing throughout its 40,000 acres. So devious are some of its channels that native guides are needed to reach many parts of it and find the way back. At no other place in Texas, where the larger percentage of the lake lies, is there comparable cypress growth. The unusually heavy growth of Spanish moss on these trees gives the lake an eerie, almost unearthly appearance.

Then there are the phenomena of strange lights in the

George Taylor

1

2

1. *A dragonfly relaxes on a double-pod cattail near the edge of Reelfoot Lake.*

2. *One of the many waterways kept clear by the Corps of Engineers as a boat trail in Caddo Lake.*

3. Miniature turtles like this one sunning on a lily pad are found at Reelfoot Lake.

4. An aerial photo of an oxbow lake created when the river abandoned its original channel and found a new one. These become swamp lakes; then, over a period of years, swamps.

5. A tiger swallowtial butterfly adds beauty to the swamp lakes. In spring, thousands of them migrate through those areas en route north.

6. One of the residents of the swamp lakes is the raccoon. Others include the opossum, red and gray fox, otter, swamp rabbit, bobcat,

and, around the drier perimeter, white-tailed deer.

7. (Overleaf) Caddo Lake.

George Taylor

5

George Taylor

6

3

George Taylor

4

swamp. Eerie lights in the middle of the night are not uncommon sights in many swamps and have been attributed to ghosts, pirates, madmen, flying saucers, and local legends. What causes these strange lights are foxfire (a luminescence given off by the decaying of wood by certain fungi), burning methane gas escaping from decomposing vegetation, or smoking, smouldering peat. It's only natural that such eerie sights become sources for many tall tales.

Each year less and less open water remains in Caddo Lake, and many of the natives claim it's dying. Because of the increase of water hyacinths and water lilies and the siltation from the backwaters of the Red River, some people who have lived in the area all their lives and have watched the changes come about predict the lake will become marsh before the year 2000.

Around the turn of the twentieth century, Caddo boomed with an influx of pearl hunters, some of whom were fortunate enough to find single pearls worth close to a thousand dollars in the lake's fresh-water mussels. A few are found yet, but the mussel population, because of earlier exploitations and lack of conservation, is sparse. Others came to Caddo to make their fortunes in oil. Oil was discovered in some parts of the lake, but it never amounted to much. Some of the old oil rigs still stand on the Louisiana side, however, rusted remainders of the lake's colorful history.

For many years after its dramatic creation, Reelfoot Lake and the area surrounding it remained a haunted wilderness which no Indian dared enter. Today, though still primitive and mysterious, it has become a major tourist attraction. Its varied and colorful vegetation, its migrating waterfowl and small animals, and its reputation as a fishing haven draw a growing number of visitors each year.

Both Caddo and Reelfoot have state parks on their shores, but Reelfoot also has two national wildlife refuges—Reelfoot and Lake Isom—nearby to accommodate migrating waterfowl along the Mississippi flyway. More than 240 species of water and land birds either live or visit here. During migration season mallards, pintails, coots, Canada geese, and other birds number in the tens of thousands. Among the small wildlife are mink, muskrat, raccoon, fox squirrel, gray squirrel, cottontail, swamp rabbit, and red fox. The fertile, stump-covered bottom of Reelfoot has promoted the growth of over 50 species of fish, and today Reelfoot is known as the nation's most productive natural fish hatchery. Largemouth bass, crappie, and bream are the most plentiful.

Reelfoot has many turtles—so many, in fact, that they have become the basis of a local industry. Each spring schoolchildren go out to net tiny turtles, hardly larger than a quarter, which they often find sunning on giant water-lily pads. The little turtles are then sold as pets in dime stores across the nation.

Like Caddo, Reelfoot is relatively shallow throughout its 15,000-acre area, averaging a depth of about twenty feet. (It, too, is diminishing in size; it once covered 30,000 acres.) The most colorful time is the early spring when the lake bursts into acres of bright yellow splotches—the

8

184

blossoms of water lilies—set on great seas of green. On the low-lying area surrounding the lake lie countless acres of smartweed, chufa, and barnyard grass, while on higher ground poison ivy, deciduous holly, blue beach, hawthorne, black gum, oak, hickory, and other southern hardwoods flourish.

Caddo and Reelfoot are by no means the only swamp lakes in America. Some of them were born in ancient river channels, abandoned by the stream in favor of a shorter, easier way to its destination. Others were created by erosion, forming deep depressions which collected drainage water. Some were created in swamps that already existed as peat fires burned great hollows in the soil. And some, more commonly referred to as oxbows, lie along rivers such as the Mississippi, the lower Ohio, and the Missouri. The oxbows vary in size, of course, but have at least one thing in common. They survive on the annual flooding of the streams from which they were created—usually in the spring—and the rest of the year remain stagnant. Along the lower hundred miles of the Ohio River, for instance, are more than a hundred such swamp lakes. The Mississippi has many times that number.

The swamp lakes, wherever you find them, occupy a unique position in the scheme of nature. First of all, by nature of their water source, they are changing more radically than the traditional swamps. For each flooding brings debris and silt to fill them. It also brings additional aquatic life including several species of fish more commonly found in rivers—catfish, carp, bream, crappie, gar, and largemouth bass. Some of the finest sport fishing in America may be found in the swamp lakes.

Since they provide such excellent habitat for certain types of fishes, they also provide excellent feeding grounds for creatures which prey upon them. Otter, mink, osprey, and numerous water snakes live in or around the swamp lake. Because they are constantly in a stage of evolution, the swamp lakes perhaps may someday within the next millennium becomes marshes or swamps in the truest sense. Both Reelfoot and Caddo already are so shallow in many parts that dense stands of cypress grow. As additional land is formed, other woody plants and vines will take root, resulting in a true swamp environment.

8. A striking sunset on Reelfoot Lake is framed with cypress stumps and knees.

CHAPTER
18
The Green Swamp

No state is under greater pressure
from all the forces that place demands upon land,
water and life . . . the United States
begins or ends in Florida.

—Raymond F. Dasmann
No Further Retreat

It was the kind of gentle spring day on which nothing could go wrong, and so the scene that was unfolding in Florida's vast Green Swamp a few miles west of Disney World seemed incongruous. Sheriff's deputies and armed members of a posse drifted through the swamp like shadows. Their quarry was a creature known only as the Wild Man of the Green Swamp. Over a period of several months, people entering or living in the swamp had reported seeing the creature or traces of its existence. There had been speculation that a Sasquatch or Skunk Ape—the mysterious Abominable Snowman of the Himalayas and of the American West—was indeed alive and roaming the Green Swamp.

When the posse converged that day in 1975 on an area deep within the swamp where a campfire had been spotted by plane, they found a small, thirty-nine-year-old recluse from Taiwan who had been living off the swamp for nearly a year, eating young alligators and armadillos, berries and wild fruit. He reported he had left his family in Taiwan to seek work in the United States, but had become frightened he might be arrested and sent home. So he escaped into the swamp to live off the land.

The fact that our Taiwan friend led such an existence is of little importance except to point up the remote qualities of one of America's least-known swamps. For even in central Florida, where it's located, many have never heard of the Green Swamp. Outside the state, few people indeed were aware of its existence. Yet it is 100 square miles larger than the Great Dismal Swamp of Virginia–North Carolina; 150 square miles larger than the Okefenokee in Georgia. The Green is the southernmost large mixed-hardwood swamp in Florida and one of the main recharge areas of the Floridian aquifer, that great flow of water southward—some surface, some subterranean—that ultimately feeds Lake Okeechobee and the Florida Everglades, as well as the Big Cypress Swamp.

Five rivers are born in the Green Swamp: the Kissimmee and Peace flowing southward; the Oklawaha north; and the Hillsborough and Withlacoochee westward.

Covering some 10,000 square miles just five miles west of Disney World, the Green Swamp is actually a swamp area, meaning not all of it is a contiguous expanse of swamp. Instead it is a composite of swamp fingers separated by flatwoods, low hills, and ridges, with an abundance of sinkhole lakes—lakes without apparent bottoms.

Much of the land, particularly the higher areas, has been utilized for grazing. Some acreage produces citrus. But about 50 percent of the swamp's remaining areas are wetlands, consisting of marshes, cypress swamps, and river swamps.

During the season when the rains come, the Green Swamp is much akin to the Big Cypress in appearance and hydrology. It drinks up the water until it becomes saturated, its pools overflowing. And then, as the dry season approaches and the rains cease, the swamp becomes a great sponge that metes out its water resources to the surrounding land. Perhaps no other swamp does so more dramatically, sending its waters in virtually every direction to sustain animals and birds, plants and people.

The Green Swamp has seldom attracted interest, and

relatively few people over the years entered the swamp to savor its unique beauty, to walk in this mostly trackless place. It is a place appreciated most by the white ibis, which floats across brassy, clouded skies to alight beside willow-shaded pools, where the stillness is broken mainly by the persistent song of the leopard frog by night and the Carolina wren by day. Pileated woodpeckers rap away at some hollow cypress trees, weathered by the elements; a raccoon clambers among the greenery to survey stands of wild orange trees in the forest below. While there are many languid pools within the swamp, there are also springs which emit a cold, sweet water from the depths of the earth.

Just exactly when the Green Swamp came to be is a matter of considerable speculation, but most agree it was sometime during the Ice Age and perhaps because of it. Although the glacier did not by any means reach Florida, it did create weather patterns which drenched the peninsula with heavy rains over long periods. Then, as the glacier retreated, the rains subsided and the area that is the Green Swamp became a grassland prairie. Slowly the vegetation of the swamp adapted to alternating patterns of the seasons: wet and dry.

The Spaniards entered this part of the Florida peninsula in the early 1500s. When their exploratory parties came to the Green Swamp, they were exhausted, and the swamp appeared even more formidable and ominous than it really was. Hawks and panthers screamed from its depths, great barred owls hooted even during the day. Overhead, black and turkey vultures soared. And the Spaniards soon left and headed north into the lands along the Suwannee River. The Green Swamp—land of raincrows and the ivory-billed woodpecker—was left to its own domain.

In 1539 scouts for Hernando De Soto, exploring Florida's timber resources for shipbuilding, entered the Green Swamp, plodding through the rich muck and wading the lettuce-choked streams. After becoming lost, they began searching for the flow of the streams to determine where they led. Finally, they found an open stretch with enough visible current to enable them to follow the flow. But they soon found they were in error, for the understory was so thick near the stream they could not follow on land. Subsequent marshes and bogs made hiking across land next to impossible. But De Soto did not believe his scouts and decided to explore the swamp himself. After much searching, he found enough high ground to cross the swamp and proceed on his expedition toward what is now Ocala.

The Green Swamp would not play another role in the annals of man until the latter half of the eighteenth century when the Seminoles began to filter into the swamp and establish villages. Within a few years they were to abandon their villages here to move farther south into the Everglades and the Big Cypress Swamps, but legends still persist. Some say if you are in the Green Swamp on a windy, moonless autumn night you can still hear the Seminole's mournful call as he is relentlessly pursued by the white man further and further into the wilderness—that and the wistful cry of the yellow-crowned night heron of which there are so many here.

1

4

2

3

1. *During the dry season, water in the Green Swamp is found only in the streams and in pools such as this one. The stumps and logs are cypress.*

2. *The trumpet or coral honeysuckle, found throughout the Green Swamp, blooms in April and produces a cluster of scarlet berries, sometimes called beans, in late autumn.*

3. *A lichen and Spanish moss, each nondependent upon the tree, grow side by side in the Green Swamp.*

4. *The beautiful Hillsborough River, born here in the Green Swamp, drains southwestward toward Tampa and the Gulf.*

Many efforts have been made by man through the years to conquer the Green Swamp, but most of them were discouraged by the dense growth, snakes, mosquitoes, and soggy earth. Most recently, grazing and wild hogs have taken their toll of the interior. The greatest threat to the swamp was the establishment in the 1960s of Disney World, just west of Orlando. While the undeveloped boundary areas of this sophisticated world of make-believe were still a good five miles away from the Green Swamp, it nevertheless brought the pressure of people and development. Real estate prices skyrocketed as resorts and campgrounds, motels and other attractions were built. It began to look as though the Green Swamp might be trampled in the onrush of tourists and land seekers.

In 1974 a $70-million project which would develop some 2,000 acres of the Green Swamp—convert it to condominium units and residential areas—was proposed. The company said it would keep 50 percent of the land in cypress stands, but that wasn't enough to satisfy many of the people who had grown to love and respect the Green Swamp. The federal government eventually became involved through the U.S. Soil Conservation Service which valued the swamp for its ability to recharge the Floridian aquifer.

If the people did not understand the need for the Green Swamp as a place of quiet retreat and a wildlife habitat, they did fully realize the increasing need for water. Ground water consumption from the Floridian aquifer is increased daily due to the addition of 6,000 or more residents to the state each week, with the majority of them settling in central and south Florida. The Green Swamp recharges some 700,000 gallons per day per square mile into the Floridian aquifer.

Gerald Parker, former chief hydrologist of the Southwest Florida Water Management District, was emphatic in his report to the people. "The Green Swamp," he said, "is invaluable to the future of water use in the state. Most of the time and over most of the area, this great natural underground storage reservoir is filled to overflowing. It supplies the enormous discharge of all the great springs of the district . . . Gourd Springs, for instance, has a discharge rate into Lake Apopka of eighteen million gallons daily . . . this is imperative to the survival of this state."

The people of Florida were convinced, and so were the members of the Florida legislature. In the summer of 1974, despite the vigorous protests of many property owners in the swamp who had purchased land with the hope of developing it at some future date, the Green Swamp was declared an area of critical state concern, which meant stringent regulations upon any type of development or use, hopefully resulting in preservation of the swamp. More than two years of effort—meetings, hearings, studies, and arguments—went into the project to achieve that stage. Still, an act of the legislature could change the status at any time, and the Green Swamp and its life-giving water might be knocked down to the highest bidder.

5. *The common egret stalks tiny fish amid cattail waters.*

6. *(Opposite) The green heron may hold this statuesque pose for hours without moving at all, then suddenly, upon spotting a fish, will dart into the water.*

Creation is still
going on. Creation is here and now . . .
—Henry Beston

The winding gravel roadway breaks into a broad tree-less vista high above the Mississippi floodplain. Directly 300 feet below, like the natural curl of a giant snake, lies the swamp, its edges framed with heavy forest. The sun's rays on this summer midday reflects glimmer of light from the carpet of duckweed on the shallow waters. Heat waves dance in the air, and a pale haze rises from its surface. A pair of redtail hawks soars overhead, searching for an unwary swamp rabbit or snake. Beyond them at higher altitude, a score of buzzards ride the thermals from the floodplain floor.

The LaRue Swamp in southern Illinois is probably the only swamp in North America maintained partially for the benefit of snakes, and poisonous ones at that. Every spring and autumn since 1973 the roads have been closed for a few days to permit the swamp's resident cottonmouth moccasins and timber rattlers safe crossing to and from their hibernation dens in the adjacent limestone rock cliffs.

While the snakes in LaRue seem to be holding their own, thanks to the new regulations, the endangered species list for the area includes a number of other unusual creatures, such as the blind spring cave fish that occupy large springs at the base of the 300-foot cliffs bordering the swamp. The rare Indiana bat lives in those cliffs, along with the eastern wood rat, and feeds over the swamp. The dwarf and pigmy sunfish are also considered rare, but are found in considerable numbers in the open waters of the swamp.

Lying along an ancient channel of the Big Muddy River, which now borders the north side of the swamp, LaRue sprawls and meanders along the main course of that abandoned channel. After the river abandoned this channel, the swamp that developed here depended upon natural drainage of rain water from the adjacent Pine Hills for its lifeblood. That wasn't enough to keep it going as long as the channel continued to drain out the lower end. But the beaver and the main channel of the river plugged the old channel, holding back the water to maintain the swamp.

Naturally, this raising of water levels has an effect upon the type of plant life growing in the swamp. Just raising the water level a foot may prove too much water for certain kinds of trees, such as the water maple or the gum, which like fluctuating levels which leave their roots dry at least a portion of each year. It may also have an effect upon types of water lilies which will only grow in a certain depth of water.

The river is kept from annually inundating the swamp by a manmade dike twenty feet wide running more than a mile along one side. Along the top of the dike is a road leading to the Pine Hills where one may get a bird's-eye view of the swamp.

It was along this ancient channel of the Big Muddy that I shoved off my canoe late one spring day, slicing the shallow silvery waters. The swamp closed behind me, and soon I was in a world lost from civilization. A pair of feeding mallards watched cautiously as I approached, then burst the silence with a flurry of wings. A green heron clucked from an unseen hideaway along the treeline. A red-shouldered hawk sat stauelike in the top of a dead tupelo gum.

1

2

1. *Mud turtles sun on a floating log near the edge of the swamp.*

2. *Even the box turtle enjoys a cooling dip at the edge of the swamp on a hot summer day.*

3. *While the cattail is more associated with marsh, many are to be found along the perimeter of LaRue Swamp.*

4. *The cottonmouth moccasin as well as the brown water snake live in LaRue Swamp.*

5. *Their season spent, these giant water lilies bear the mark of frost as winter draws high.*

3

5

4

6

7

6. *The LaRue Swamp actually is an ancient channel of the Big Muddy River which borders it to the north. Upon the horizon is the Mississippi River.*

7. *Along the higher ground, several species of ferns grow, including the Christmas fern.*

8. *Farther into the swamp, the duckweed gives way to occasional pools which harbor largemouth bass, bream, catfish, and crappie.*

8

As I glided silently along, fish jumped around me, feeding on tiny flying insects just above the surface. A water snake left a faint wake as it crossed just twenty feet in front of my canoe. It was almost as though I belonged here.

As the canoe neared a small knoll rising out of the water, a snapping turtle the size of a frying pan sprung into the water. And all along the way a symphony of bird songs—mockingbirds, Carolina wrens, redwings, cardinals, thrushes, combined with the unique bird-voiced tree frog—accompanied the splash of my paddle. As the evening drew on, the symphony was joined by the deep-throated croak of the bullfrog.

I was maneuvering the canoe to swing back to my starting point when suddenly, out of the willow trees, there was a startling rush of wings, and a great barred owl swooped low overhead, then disappeared into the sun. A fat cottonmouth writhed through the water only five feet away from the canoe, and another, just to starboard, laced its way toward me broadside. I raised my paddle in a defense I hoped I would not have to use as he swam alongside, placed his triangular head against the canoe and started up. I could see the pits just forward of the slitted eyes, the tongue working feverishly.

Just as I was about to bring the wooden paddle down hard upon his skull, he dived straight down and under, coming up ten feet away on the other side. I decided he was just curious about this new intruder in his domain, and satisfied this was nothing he could eat, he had gone his way.

If I had entertained any thoughts about spending the night in the swamp before, I certainly had none now, and I sped up the channel toward Winter Pond, as a gold quarter-moon hung over the Pine Bluffs treetops. The water had turned a dull black except for the moonpath, and the night creatures were stirring. The swamp, any swamp, is really two worlds—one that lives by night, the other by day. And when it comes to swamps, I am a day creature.

When I returned to LaRue Swamp, it was late October. The snakes had gone to bed for the winter somewhere in the rock cliffs, the geese and ducks (mallards and mergansers) had begun to migrate down the Mississippi flyway from colder northern climes, and the trees had shed most of their leaves. The water lilies, which last spring were just emerging from the swamp floor, now lay in giant pads flush with the water, their edges fringed a crusty brown from an early frost. The swamp had grown silent—it was about to go to sleep for the winter. The raccoons, the opossum, the red and gray foxes, the squirrels, and the skunks would be around during most of the winter, as would the beavers; but the sounds of an exuberant awakening were gone. The cycle of another year was nearly complete.

Although there are numerous river overflow swamps up and down the Mississippi all the way from Minnesota to southern Louisiana, as well as on the lower Ohio and Missouri Rivers, LaRue Swamp has special qualities. When U.S. Regional Forester Lyle Watts visited the area in 1937, he initiated special regulations for the protection and reestablishment of the original character of this place.

It was then called the LaRue Botanical Area, later to become a Scenic Area under a new Forest Service classification. Not until the 1960s, when university studies were published, was the scientific value of the swamp actually realized.

Over one-third of all Illinois plants, including more than 40 species that have been declared rare in this area, can be found here because of the protected and remote status of the swamp. Some of these include the shortleaf pine, wild azalea, and red iris. There are southern swamp cypress, tupelo gum, sweet gum, sassafras, sycamore, maple, beech, and a variety of oaks. Some 40 mammal, 24 amphibian, 35 reptile, and 173 bird species have been sighted within its boundaries, including all the animals normally found in southern Illinois and several rare species. In winter, American bald eagle frequent the area, but have never been known to nest here.

Today, students and scientists from universities and other institutions across America utilize the swamp for field research on some of these rare species. At one time, they did extensive collecting which nearly left the swamp sterile, resulting in U.S. Forest Service regulations banning the collection of certain species and dramatically limiting others. And in 1970, the swamp was designated a part of the LaRue–Pine Hills Ecological Area, the first such designation in the entire national forest system, which further insures the conservation of those species.

9

9. *Among the waterfowl inhabitants is the coot, which migrates along the Mississippi.*

10. *Leaves of a nearby black oak tree lie sprinkled upon black waters reflecting a late autumn sun.*

10

Cottongrass in Cranberry Bog, W. Va.

CHAPTER
20
Mountain Swamps of the East

Every part of this soil is
sacred in the estimation of my people.
Every hillside, every valley,
every plain and grove . . .
—Chief Seattle

There is an extraordinary variety in the wetlands of America, depending upon their location, physical environment, and geological origin. Some are found in the lowlands, saucers which are filled from surrounding terrain, while others are found on domes from which the water flows outward. Some are called sloughs, some bogs, marshes, or swamps. Their similarites have been touched on previously in this book, and yet they are all quite distinct. We come now to a category of wetlands in which all the distinguishing guidelines seem to break down: the mountain swamps of the east.

From the Smokies northward to Canada, bogs and swamps are plentiful at higher altitudes. For instance, there are at least 40,000 wetland areas within the Adirondacks covering an estimated 512,000 acres. In the Applachians of east Tennessee, Kentucky, western Virginia, West Virginia, Maryland, and Pennsylvania are uncharted swamps and bogs far too numerous to count. The majority of them are relatively small, certainly when compared with the major swamps of the southern states, but they play an integral role in the ecological character of alpine areas and offer perhaps a unique beauty in sharp seasonal contrasts.

While many of the wetlands found in the lower Appalachians and Blue Ridge Mountains are generally sphagnum and cranberry bogs, many other mountain swamps extending northward into the Adirondacks, the White Mountains of New Hampshire, and on into Maine are dominated by a boreal forest largely composed of black and red spruce, balsam fir, and tamarack and such shrubs as Labrador tea, bog rosemary, and wild cranberries.

The base of many of the Adirondack swamps is limestone, with a peat layer of varying depths. They are usually found in valleys, along the perimeter of lakeside meadows or near gentle, slow-moving streams. They may encompass plant life indicative of the marsh and bog as well as wooded species associated with the swamp environment. For instance, cattails and spike rushes may be quite common to many of the Adirondack swamps, but you'll also find black alder, maple, aspen, spruce, and tamarack.

Because many of the mountain swamps of the Adirondacks provide shrubby browse and shelter from winter storms, they make excellent cover for white-tailed deer. Many such swamps are dense along their perimeters, but inside open up into rooms roofed by great hemlocks, tamarack, and white cedar. If you enter these areas quietly and employ some good stalking techniques, you may see some of the other wild inhabitants too—otter, beaver, bobcat, weasel, raccoon, and even mink. Birds are plentiful, and sometimes you may flush a spruce grouse. The reptile population in the mountain swamp is perhaps less than in any other type of wetland. Only a few salamanders, frogs, eastern box turtles, rare northern bog turtles, and perhaps an occasional northern water snake are found here. Stand or sit quietly—this takes much patience—and your chances of seeing wildlife are much improved.

But if you find few of these wild creatures, you most likely will find an abundance of mosquitoes. For the

1

2

1. *Interrupted fern from the mountain swamps of the Adirondacks.*

2. *False hellebore grows along the edges of swamps in the Adirondacks.*

3. *Purple trillium.*

4. *In the spring, catkins emerge, providing food for some kinds of birds.*

3

4

5. *(Overleaf) At Dolly Sods, W. Va., is a true northern bog more typical of those found in the Canadian arctic.*

greatest breeding grounds for mosquitoes are not in the tropical swamps, but in the subarctic regions of the north. And since the mountain swamps more closely resemble the arctic regions than they do the tropics, you naturally find plenty of mosquitoes. The sphagnum moss provides an excellent breeding ground for mosquitoes; it not only protects them from birds and other predatory insects, but it affords them a damp, dark haven away from the direct sunlight. As the sun fades in the evening, the mosquitoes emerge from the moss to feed.

During the warm summer months, the density of mosquitoes is heaviest, which makes this season the worst time of year to visit the mountain swamps. If you have doubts where the mosquitoes are, step lightly upon the moss and watch the clouds of these insects emerge. Not all mosquitoes bite, of course. Only the female possesses the equipment necessary for sucking blood. Their prey is not only man, but all types of animals and certain species of insects as well.

The rare and endangered spruce grouse, the American and arctic three-toed woodpeckers, brown-capped chickadees, gray jays, and the Lincoln sparrow also live here. The spruce grouse most often occupies poorly drained black spruce–balsam fir–larch forests. Such bog forests are often edged by a heath mat of blueberry, Labrador tea, leather-leaf, and sheep and bog laurels. The bog habitat most suited to the spruce grouse lies roughly between 1,400-and 1,800-foot elevation. Virtually all the boreal species of birds mentioned, however, are migrant with the exception of the three-toed arctic woodpecker and the spruce grouse. By early June when the bog laurel and bog rosemary are in full bloom, the birds living in the boreal wetlands have begun nesting and the forest is alive with their music.

One of the most representative swamps in the Adirondacks is Jones Pond Swamp near Saranac Lake, and the best way to see it is by canoe. For a true mountain swamp experience, paddle down Jones Pond outlet crossing Osgood Pond to about a mile below its outlet. Here the spruce-tamarack swamp crowded close on both sides suddenly breaks away, leaving a pristine sphagnum bog on the west side. Farther along at the confluence of Blind Brook, one can venture out on a primitive muskeg wilderness clumped with white-fringed orchids.

Approximately 100 miles south of Jones Pond, the Cranesville Swamp lies across the hilly border of Maryland and West Virginia. Some 300 of the swamp's original 560 acres are owned and preserved by the Nature Conservancy, but a good bit of the swamp has been destroyed by farming and logging operations. To this day, parts of the swamp are gradually being converted to farmland.

What is left is precious, for it represents one of the few remaining ''northern bogs'' in the southern states. The formation of Cranesville Swamp probably began some 10,000 to 25,000 years ago during the Pleistocene age. Although none of the four major advances of the glacier reached the Cranesville region, the prevailing climatic conditions at that time had a profound effect upon the swamp.

The boreal forest, consisting mainly of spruce and tamarack, stretches across the continent just south of the

6. *Dewberry or groundberry, as it's sometimes called, at Cranesville Swamp.*

7. *Snow gives an appropriate tone to Christmas fern in Cranesville Swamp.*

8. *Wild cranberries peek through an early snowfall at Cranesville Swamp.*

7

8

tundra in Canada and Alaska. When the glaciers began to move south, the forest fell back southward ahead of them. When the glaciers retreated northward, the boreal forest followed, and the eastern deciduous forest gradually moved northward to occupy its original position. In a few locations such as Cranesville, pockets of the boreal forest were left behind.

The boreal forest climate also prevails at Cranesville, for it may snow as much as eight or nine months of the year. In fact, it was snowing in late September when I took a day-long hike into the swamp. Colorful autumn leaves still clung to the deciduous trees, the wild cranberries and sphagnum moss had turned red and gold and brown, presenting a dramatic contrast to the wet snow that quickly crystallized upon them.

Between the flurries that marched under ominous clouds across the swamp were breaks of clear blue mountain skies and sunshine, melting the crystals into rivulets that ran in steady streams from the leaves into the spongy peat soil. Ultimately it would find its way to Muddy Creek which runs through the area, providing an overflow for the swamp.

Dr. Roy B. Clarkson of West Virginia University's Department of Biology notes three primary factors favoring the boreal atmosphere of the swamp. One is a comparatively cool regional climate with short growing seasons resulting from the 2,500-foot altitude; another is the natural frost pocket produced by the bowl-shaped valley in which the swamp lies. A third is the poor drainage of water from the area which makes it unfavorable for common species, thus allowing the boreal species to continue their growth. Otherwise, he feels the boreal forest would long ago have been crowded out—as it was in other areas—by deciduous forest growth.

Geologists believe Cranesville Swamp was born when Muddy Creek, the main drainage stream, cut down to a resistant layer of rock called the Pottsville Conglomerate. This rock was so hard it resisted the downward cutting of the water, thereby preventing good drainage. The water stood, and mosses and lichens grew, sponging up the water and holding it. Peat began to form and today in some places reaches a depth of five feet. Many of the great trees achieved a faster growth rate with the availability of mineral-rich water. But time would see their demise at the hands of man.

About 1870 the logging industry in the Cranesville area began to develop, and the swamp was just one of the places the loggers headed. White pine were the first to be cut. When these were gone, the woodsmen turned to hemlock and chestnut oak, walnut, cherry, yellow poplar, and white oak from the periphery. In 1891 a narrow-gauge railroad was built into Cranesville or Piney Swamp, as the locals called it, and a Climax steam locomotive named the Swamp Angel began hauling logs to a sawmill at Rinard (now Hopemont), West Virginia.

In October, 1960, the Nature Conservancy purchased the first parcel of the swamp—259 acres. Since then additional purchases plus some donations were made, and this land was formally dedicated as the Cranesville Swamp Nature Sanctuary.

The swamp is a botanical mecca with cinnamon fern, skunk cabbage, royal fern, arrowleaf, purple trillium, laurel, rhododendron, appalachian tea, black chokeberry, winterberry, mountain holly, and creeping snowberry. Wild cranberries found here are of the same species as those grown commercially in the northeast. When I visited the swamp, the cranberries were ripe for picking and open meadows of the swamp were dotted with cottongrass, a sedge found in several mountain swamps of the east. This is the type of environment necessary for the growth of Harned's swamp clintonia, a species resembling the white clintonia. The late Dr. Joseph Harned, a pharmacist in Oakland, Md., and author of *Wildflowers of the Al-leghenies,* was the discoverer of this rare plant.

Aside from botanical growth, there are interesting species of wildlife as well, starting with some of the lower-form salamanders and blue montane crayfish. In the creek are found northern creek chub. At one time there were native rainbow and brook trout here, but no longer—fishermen have taken the last of them. Snowshoe hare, cottontail rabbit, beaver, raccoon, bobcat, gray and red fox, white-tailed deer, and the northern water shrew all live in Cranesville Swamp. Once there were wolf and black bear here.

A hundred miles further south is a mountain bog similar in many ways to Cranesville. Located in the Monongahela National Forest, it's known as Cranberry Glades, an area of approximately 750 acres surrounded by Cranberry, Kennison, and Black Mountains.

The most unusual features of the Glades are the areas of open bog and peatland. Such bogs, popularly known in West Virginia as glades, are not at all rare, but this particular one is by far the most extensive and the best preserved. Located some 3,400 feet above sea level, the Glades is fed by springs which actually are the origin of the Cranberry River.

Speckled alder, dwarf dogwood, oak fern, goldthread, bog rosemary, and buckbean are found here, as well as wild cranberries. Found here also are three carnivorous plants—the sundew, horned bladderwort, and the pitcher plant. The latter was introduced and is not native to West Virginia, however. Elderberry, wild grape, mountain holly, arrowwood, yew, chokeberry, and St. John's wort, as well as skunk cabbage, marsh marigold, jack-in-the-pulpit, wild rose, wood sorrel, golden ragwort, monk's hood, and various ferns and asters grow here.

A boardwalk leads through the Glades. The earth floor appears solid, but if there's doubt in your mind, test it with one foot while keeping the other on the boardwalk. You sink into the cold ooze well above your shoetop and the sphagnum moss closes around your leg. At several points in the scrub-tree sections of the bog are running brooks, carrying away the waters as the bog slopes some forty-five feet to the west.

Dr. H. C. Darlington, who did extensive studies on the Cranberry Glades, believes the level area of the Glades developed as the consequence of a pattern of differential surface erosion. Measurements show that from the top of Cranberry Mountain to the bog area, a distance of three miles, the dip of the slope is 275 feet per mile, while for the next five miles down the Cranberry River the dip is

9. *A small swamp typical of several found in the mountain areas of Maine. This one is located in Baxter State Park.*

only 125 feet a mile. In other words, the rushing water cut deep into the riverbed upstream, but as it slowed and spread out on more resistant rockbed in the Glades, it created a marsh or bog area. Here the streams cut sideways in the softer top layers of rock, spreading out to unusual widths.

Peat covers much of the area, but not all of it. In the areas of extensive peat deposits, an analysis was made which showed that it took as much as 9,423 years to build the twelve-foot depth attained there.

Many other alpine swamps and bogs exist throughout the eastern mountain chain, including Blister Swamp only a few miles away, Canaan Valley, some small bogs in the Dolly Sods Wilderness Area near Petersburg, W. Va., and thousands of swamps and bogs in the Green Mountains of Vermont, the White Mountains of New Hampshire, and Maine. Many of them exhibit great similarites to either Cranberry Glades or Cranesville Swamp; thus these two serve as representative examples.

10

10. In many of the mountain swamps is found Polytrichum *moss, shown here in bloom.*

11. Sphagnum moss holds water like a sponge. It is found in mountain swamps from Maine to the southern Appalachians.

12. Black chokeberry, which is quite tasty, grows profusely in Cranesville Swamp.

11

CHAPTER
21
Swamps around You

Hope and the future for me
are not in lawns and cultivated fields, not in towns
and cities, but in the impervious and
quaking swamps . . . that was
the jewel which dazzled me.

—Thoreau

The State of Michigan has as its state motto: "If you seek a pleasant peninsula, look about you." Several states, including Michigan, might paraphrase that motto: "If you seek a tranquil swamp, look around you." For swamps, marshes, and bogs are located in some degree in virtually every state.

Granted there are more of these natural phenomena in some areas than in others. North and South Carolina, Florida, Louisiana, and Texas have the greatest number; there are considerable numbers in Minnesota, Wisconsin, Michigan, Mississippi, Arkansas, and Georgia. A few marshes and bogs can be found even in Arizona and New Mexico, considered the most arid states in the entire country. The U.S. Fish and Wildlife Service, in evaluating wetlands useful for waterfowl, lists more than 28,000 acres in Arizona and 48,000 acres in New Mexico. Undoubtedly there are additional bogs and marshes that aren't rated under that agency's report.

How often we look, but fail to see. One day in 1974 after I had been assigned to do this book, I began to notice swamps and marshes along the New York Thruway. I had driven that multi-lane highway many times during the past ten years and had not noted a single swamp or marsh. Now the countryside was suddenly filled with them. One might think they were placed there just yesterday.

Some of them were not large; in fact, a good many would not cover an acre. But they possessed all the characteristics I had come to associate with swamps and marshes. Woody plants grew in and around some of them, as well as the familiar cattails and spike grass and rushes. Mosses and lichens and algae grew profusely from the banks and in the shallow water. On some, wood ducks swam, and occasionally a pair of mallards sprang from the open places to disappear into the June sky.

At Utica, heading west, I began to count. By the time I had reached Buffalo, I had spotted more than 200. Some of them exceeded, in my estimation, ten acres in size; but the majority were smaller. I was amazed that there should be so many.

From that time on, I began to do a bit of swamp watching as I drove around the country. Surprisingly, I found that almost everywhere I went, there were within plain view wetlands of various types—swamps, bogs, sloughs, marshes.

In my own home state of Indiana, for instance, there are more than twenty swamps, marshes, and bogs exceeding 15 acres, some as large as 200 acres. Although most are on private land, they are being preserved in a near pristine state by the families who own them. Among them is Cabin Creek Bog, one of four known inland raised bogs in America. The others are located in Ohio, Minnesota, and Yellowstone National Park. This one happens to be approximately ten feet above the surrounding land in southern Indiana, with artesian waters springing from near its center and flowing outward in virtually every direction.

Marshes occur mostly in the western United States and along the eastern coastal areas. The salt marshes which lie along the east coast of North America begin in the north as grassy arctic marshes on Baffin Island and Hudson Bay, as well as along the upper reaches of Labrador. Southward from Maine and New England they spread sporadically down the coast, a gradual transformation from grassy marshes to the mangrove swamps of Florida. Occasionally one finds swamps close to the sea, also. One of the most beautiful swamps I've seen anywhere is located in the Cape Cod National Seashore area of Massachusetts. It's small but impressive, and a boardwalk has been constructed through its midst to allow visitors the opportunity to experience some of its flavor without endangering the swamp.

Hawaii has several bogs, swamps, and marshes; Alaska is covered with vast bogs (no swamps), but so unexplored is the state that even by 1975 most of those bogs had not been charted. Other major states having extensive wetland acreage include Florida, with some 17 million acres; Louisiana, 9.6 million; Minnesota, 5 million; Arkansas, 3.7 million; North Carolina, 4 million; South Carolina, 3.3 million; Texas, 3.7 miliion; Michigan, 3.2 million; Wisconsin, 2.7 million; Alabama, 1.6 million; and Utah, 1.1 million acres, the latter mostly in marsh.

New Hampshire has so many bogs, marshes, and swamps it doesn't keep tabs on them, and New York in the early part of this century was in the business of building swamps and marshes. Through 1955, the state had created more than 600 marshes and swamps, averaging four to five acres in size, primarily in the interest of providing waterfowl habitat. Some of them were probably among those I spotted from the New York Thruway.

The point is that, wherever you live, chances are good there's a swamp, marsh, bog, or slough located within a couple of hours driving time from home. It may be small and at first glance seem insignificant. But there's plenty to see there if you know how to look. Renowned naturalist Ernest Thompson Seton spent a great deal of his time in the wilds just sitting perfectly still on a rock or backed up against a tree. By moving nothing except his eyes, he appeared to the wild creatures around him to belong, and they moved into full view where he could study their movements.

I personally have employed this technique many times and find it works remarkably well. Once when sitting on the edge of a swamp against a tree, I heard something running toward me in the woods. Soon it was within close range—an adult red fox. It easily loped along until it came to within ten feet of me. Suddenly it stopped, stared at me, licked its chops, twitched its ears, then circled cautiously a few feet, stopped again facing me, and then circled again a few more feet. Satisfied I was harmless, it edged to within six feet and stood staring at me. I stared back. I moved not a muscle, and soon the fox was convinced I either belonged there or would do him no harm. It lay down, scratched the side of its head as a dog would do and walked around a bit. Then, as though bored with this stonelike creature it had discovered in its domain, it continued on its way.

Often your entry into the swamp disturbs its wild creatures, who then fall silent. If you make no noise and do not stir, the swamp will come to life within minutes.

If you spend enough time in wild places, you'll soon learn the regulations by which you must abide. They are

214

1

2

1. A male redwing blackbird stands closeby, guarding a nest on which his mate incubates three eggs. Often seen in smaller swamps as well as larger ones, they are easily observed, particularly during nesting.

2. Baby redwings await the return of their mother with food. This nest was built among the blades of cattail on the edge of a small swamp in Indiana.

3. A good example of the diversity of plant life found in the smaller swamps.

4. Some swamps have open pools bordered by dense underbrush.

5. If you live in an area extending from Florida to the northwest territories of Canada, you may see this type of pitcher plant in swamps or bogs close to home. It eats insects by attracting them with a sweet odor into the leaf-like tubes.

6. Milkweed pods and leaves.

5

6

considered good woodsmanship. The swamp is no different. To enter is to introduce a foreigner into its midst, and your presence most certainly will be felt. But you can minimize the effects by avoiding damage to the swamp environment. I seldom break a twig; if I turn a log to study the creatures living under it, I always return it to its original position before moving on. Avoid littering the waters or the land and leave nothing but footprints. Even then, by wearing tennis shoes or sneakers, you'll do less damage trampling than you would with heavy boots or hard-soled shoes. Remember the swamp is a fragile environment. Treat it gingerly.

Little more equipment is needed for exploring most swamps than you would use to explore any wild remote place. In some swamps, such as the Florida Everglades or the Big Cypress, one can experience them best by hiking. But in swamps such as the Four Holes of South Carolina or the Atchafalaya, a canoe is an ideal craft. In fact, it's virtually the only way to experience some swamps. Any canoe will do, but usually the shorter the better, so one can weave through tight turns with less difficulty. Always take two items with you—a snakebite kit and a first-aid kit. I also carry some food supplies—usually some apples and candy bars—and unless you are sure of safe, usable water from the swamp, a jug or canteen of water. A hunting knife and flashlight are also part of my swamp equipment, just in case I should have to spend the night. An insect repellent is often a must.

No special clothes are needed for swamp wear. Tennis shoes are best for hiking and wading through most waters during warm season; otherwise, you may want to use chest waders or hip boots. Any old clothes that are tear resistant and will protect you from briars—blue denims or Army khakis or similar material—are fine. It's a good idea to wear a long-sleeved shirt in swamps infested with mosquitoes. I find wearing a T-shirt under my shirt protects against mosquito bites even more, for they often can bite through one layer of clothing. I always take a poncho and a change of clothes packed in a waterproof plastic bag on trips of several hours' duration.

Swamps are full of surprises, not all of them pleasant. For instance, Bayou Boeuf Swamp near Alexandria, La., contains tarantulas and scorpions. They are found in the drier section, primarily in the rolling piney woods. Some of the big hairy tarantulas are almost three inches in length, but they, like many residents of the swamp, are harmless. They just look scary.

The more you visit the swamp, the more you'll notice. Upon your first visit, you may overlook many of the smaller life forms. As you become better acquainted with the swamp, you see the insects, the plants, the amphibians, the birds, the reptiles. Soon you will find an entire new world opening up for you, for the swamp is just that—a world unto itself.

Morning glories.

CHAPTER
22

How to Build Your Own Swamp

Spring had just begun to creep north past the upper Mississippi marshlands and sprawling river valley just south of St. Paul, Minnesota, when the neighborhood was aroused early one morning by the clatter of a bulldozer and dragline excavating a gaping hole in Alice Bradford's back yard. All day the giant machines worked, scooping out the sand and clay mixture, sloping the banks and leveling off the bottom. When curious neighbors asked Mrs. Bradford if she were building another house, she answered cheerfully: "Nope, we're building a swamp."

Nobody in his right mind would build a swamp in Minnesota. To the neighbors, as to most people, swamps meant mosquitoes, snakes, a quagmire to be avoided. But Mrs. Bradford had grown up close to a swamp, had spent many hours of her life meditating in the swamp or along its edge, and she could think of no better way to enhance her enjoyment of life than to have her very own swamp in her very own back yard.

What she hopes will eventually be a full-fledged swamp initially appeared as a shallow pond. After a few months, during which Mrs. Bradford sought out and transferred plants from other swamps, the pond looked less like a pond and more like a swamp.

Building a swamp in your backyard isn't a simple process by any means; neither is it inexpensive. Mrs. Bradford figures she has invested more than $2,000 in her small swamp. The hours of labor that went into the Bradford Swamp haven't been tabulated, but they would run into the thousands. When you love swamps, however, you count neither effort nor expense.

The Bradford Swamp doesn't play an important ecological role in that area south of St. Paul. It may contribute a few mosquitoes to an area already heavily infested with them. It provides a stopping place for a few wild ducks from time to time, attracts a few more song birds and other wildlife than normally would be the case. Deer, raccoon, mallard, bluewing teal, and dragonflies visit occasionally. And it provides habitat for some bullfrogs and spring creepers, and a botanical garden including arrowhead, water lilies, cattails, river birch, sugar maples, Russian olive, balsam, and sumac.

Since there are numerous small swamps and marshes in Minnesota, there is no real ecological need for the Bradford Swamp. To Mrs. Bradford, though, the swamp is invaluable, and it may help to replace another swamp that was once located nearby. When Mr. and Mrs. Bradford moved here thirty years ago, a swamp on an adjacent plot backed up on the rear of the Bradford land. The neighbor didn't like swamps, however, and proceeded to drain it. When he drained his own land, he drained as well the portion which was on the Bradford acreage. That's when Alice Bradford decided to build her own. Her first effort was a failure. She had a hole dug and lined it with heavy plastic, then covered the plastic with a layer of earth. Unfortunately, the tractor punctured the plastic while putting down the earth layer, and as a result the "swamp" wouldn't hold water.

She then consulted everyone she knew who was knowledgeable about swamps and ponds, and ultimately got in touch with the U.S. Soil Conservation Service which provides free assistance on such projects. Local offices are located in most cities throughout the country and are listed in the telephone directory.

"The SCS was most helpful in recommending how to go about it," recalled Mrs. Bradford. "We found a lot of people with a lot of different ideas on just what a swamp should be and what it should look like. So we took what we felt were good recommendations and struck out on our own. We had to pump water into the swamp to fill it, but now, except in extremely dry periods, rainwater is sufficient to maintain it."

If you decide to build your own swamp you should select a site which will be most practical for your purposes. Once the site is selected, it's good to have the County Agricultural Extension Agent study the soil. Clay soils hold water much better than sandy ones. Mrs. Bradford's soil happened to have a clay loam substructure which allows water seepage, so measures had to be taken to restrict the loss of water.

The slopes of the swamp were excavated with a one-foot drop every five feet away from the edge. Then Bentonite (a type of clay) was mixed into the top six inches of the swamp floor at the rate of about one pound per square foot. This mixture of soil and Bentonite created a moisture barrier that keeps the swamp water from seeping away.

Mrs. Bradford's construction of a swamp is relatively simple compared to some swamp projects. In the Kissimmee River Valley of Florida, it appears that vast swamplands will have to be restored in order to preserve the ecological balance of Lake Okeechobee and maintain the purity of south Florida's drinking water. Since the swamplands along the river naturally cleansed pollutants from the waters before they reached Lake Okeechobee, as mentioned in an earlier chapter of this book, it has become vitally important that the swamplands which once were an integral part of the river's ecological system be restored. As of 1975 the Florida Division of State Planning and the U.S. Corps of Engineers hadn't settled on a definite course of action, but they were positive of two things. First, reflooding was totally within the realm of possibility; second, it would be extremely expensive.

On the campus of the University of Southwestern Louisiana at Lafayette is an excellent example of what can be done when one wishes to build a swamp. Although it is known locally as Cypress Lake, the area alongside the Student Union Building has all the characteristics of a Louisiana Cypress swamp—and it was developed from a pig pen. Long before that, it is believed to have been a buffalo wallow. According to the late Ira S. Nelson, who did geologic studies of the swamp, it was created by fighting buffalo bulls and further developed by wallowing buffalo.

"The bulls pounded the turf of the soft, swamplike soil prior to the time this part of Louisiana was settled," Nelson said. Great herds of them roamed the Attakapas plains area which stretches for miles just west of Lafayette. The depressions left by the fighting buffalo were quickly filled by rivulets of rain water, and soon a pond was formed. There were many of them on the Attakapas plains, and they came to be called "bull holes" or, as the Acadians referred to them, "trous de taureau."

1

2

3

1. A single cattail head provides enough seed to raise this many cattails . . . and more. Just spread them by hand around the edge of the water in the early spring.

2. A week after beginning construction, Alice Bradford's Minnesota swamp looked like this; but two years later it was surrounded by willows, arrowhead, cattails, and was home to frogs, turtles, snakes, and a pair of mallards.

When the university was established, the swamp was a pig pen operated as part of a dairy and hog farm. When the university purchased the farm, the pig pen was removed. Former President Joel Fletcher, who was on the faculty of the College of Agriculture in the early 1920s, said he had the pigs and the barn moved, drained the area and cleaned it up. What had been a buffalo wallow and pig pen now became Cypress Grove and was used as an open-air theatre where traveling Shakespearean troupes performed. Dance classes were held here, too, as well as commencement exercises.

During World War II, however, there was concern that the university might be shut off from its piped-in water supply, so Cypress Swamp was filled with water. Besides, members of the College of Agriculture faculty thought the lack of water during previous years might prove harmful to the great bald cypress trees that had stood there for centuries. A pump was installed and water pumped into the depression.

"This is called a lake on campus," said Dr. T. J. Arceneau of the College of Agriculture, "but it's really a natural Louisiana swamp. We'd like to use it as such, and long-range plans call for placing in it all of the woody plants and many of the herbaceous plants found in Louisiana swamp areas." He pointed out that it is necessary to travel about the state to find all the different varieties of swamp growth, but Cypress Swamp today provides habitat for the garfish and the alligator, the mute swan and the great blue heron.

For a time the swamp was used as a test site for growing and experimentation with Louisiana wild iris, but in 1955 the project was discontinued. However, some of the more beautiful Louisiana native iris still grow here, along with numerous other swamp plantings transferred to this location. These include sweet bay, red bay, red maple, Carolina ash, dahoon, palmetto, American sweet olive, water tupelo, titi, buttonbush, spider lilies, wild rice, climbing fern, and wild azalea.

Most of these were transplanted under a project directed by Dr. S. L. Solymosy, professor of horticultural research. "It was a simple matter," he said. "Soil conditions were similar to much of that found in Louisiana swamps. We merely dug the plants up at other locations, along with a ball of their native soil, brought them here and planted them. The mortality rate was very small."

Mrs. Bradford likewise has experienced little difficulty in getting plants to grow in her swamp. "I have an abundance of cattails," she said, "and they all came from the seeds of one cattail head which I broke off at maturity. I spread the seeds myself. The water lilies we had to transplant."

She warned, however, that one must take care not to transfer plants from one climatic zone to another or from one type of swamp to another. "We've found that plants do best," she said, "when transferred from nearby swamps, no more than fifty miles away. Of course, we're lucky that Minnesota has an abundance of such swamps convenient to us."

Once you've established certain plant species, you'll find others will often show up automatically. Birds and waterfowl carry certain types of aquatic growth.

4

5

3. *Your swamp may attract interesting insects, too, such as this praying mantis.*

4. *Spike grasses and rushes may adapt to your swamp naturally, their seeds transported and planted by birds or the winds.*

5. *Add a touch of artistry to your swamp by throwing an old log or two into shallow water.*

Duckweed, for instance, whether you want it or not, will often be transplanted by migrating ducks and geese. An abundance of fish will soon bring otter and raccoon, if there are any living in the neighborhood. Swamp rabbits may also be attracted to your swamp if there is sufficient food and cover. Frogs, salamanders, and snakes will discover your swamp, too, and come to live there.

The folks at Jaffrey, N.H., could tell you a lot about what is involved in building a swamp or a marsh. They built their own community marsh just outside town. Actually, it was first created by a colony of beaver, but the dam holding back the brook was washed away during heavy rains back in the early 1960s. The marsh—an area of only a few acres—is part of a 220-acre private estate owned by the heirs of Rear Admiral and Mrs. Mary Ainsworth Greene.

In early 1963, an earthen dam was built using plans from the U.S. Soil Conservation Service, and in no time there were lots of horned-pout and pickerel weed growing. Willows sprung up along the banks, and lilies began to grow in the shallow water. The marsh has been opened to considerate use by the more than 3,000 residents of Jaffrey, among them fishermen, hunters, and birdwatchers. Muskrat and beaver live there, and birdwatchers may see sparrows, finches, flycatchers, thrushes, and a host of migrant warblers. Lady-slippers, marsh marigolds, and trout lilies grow profusely. Mink, otter, and wood duck often are seen in the marsh.

Norman Torrey, whose wife is one of the heirs to the property on which the marsh is located, said in a local newspaper article: "We consider the marsh a boon not only to the Greene heirs, but to the whole community." Hardly a resident in all of Jaffrey would disagree.

"Developing your own swamp is like witnessing creation," said Alice Bradford. "You start from scratch with a hole in the ground, add water, encourage plant life and then let nature take its course. It doesn't happen overnight; it usually takes years. We don't expect it to become a full-fledged swamp or bog overnight. If it did, we wouldn't enjoy it half so much."

Dr. Don Whitehead of Indiana University believes the ideal situation for a project of this type would be to have a small stream flowing through the area in which you plan to create a swamp. Scooping out of the earth and allowing the stream to spread shallow over a broad surface will create the water base for a swamplike project. This way, the swamp has water flowing in and water flowing out. It would help if the outlet of the stream were altered to a location other than the original one so the water's current may be slowed as it enters the swamp. But the flow should be maintained. Then introduce your plants, your fish, and whatever other creatures you think would like this place for a home. It helps, of course, if you have a peat base in the soil. If you have plenty of money to spend, you might purchase peat and spread it six to twelve inches deep over the entire area before you add water. Sprinkle it with a garden hose so it will pack down firmly and there will be little erosion.

You may want to add commercial fertilizer to promote aquatic plant growth. That will depend some upon soil tests which you should make through the Soil Conserva-

tion Service or your County Agricultural Extension Service. Either of these government agencies can advise you on this matter, free of charge.

In two to four years you will notice, if your swamp develops a healthy environment, an increase in wildlife population, provided your swamp is not too pressured by the presence of people. Then one day, when you see redwing blackbirds nesting in the cattails and watch them raise their young, when you can hardly hear in the spring for the symphony of frogs, when you watch a great blue heron or a green heron alight and spend a few days, you will know you have succeeded in building your own swamp.

6. Unless you live in the South, getting cypress knees like this to appear in your swamp may be difficult, but they do add considerable beauty.

7. Once you've established your swamp, you may be able to attract various types of wildlife and waterfowl, such as these swans on the USL campus.

8. At the University of Southwestern Louisiana campus at Lafayette is Cypress Lake, constructed from a pig pen during World War II.